TRAP

Eden Robinson

lines

Alfred A. Knopf
Canada

PUBLISHED BY ALFRED A. KNOPF CANADA

Copyright © 1996 by Eden Robinson

Canadian Cataloguing in Publication Data
Robinson, Eden
Traplines

ISBN 0-394-28194-2

I. Title.

PS8585.035143T73   1996   CB13'.54   C96-930493-5
PR9199.3.R533T73

First Canadian Edition

Printed and bound in the United States of America
Printed on acid-free paper. ∞

To John and Winnie Robinson

Some people believe that unborn souls
choose their parents.

I'm glad I chose such gentle, loving people.

ACKNOWLEDGMENTS

I take full responsibility for these stories but happily admit that a good part of their polish comes from tireless editing by people such as Bill Valgardson, Mark Jarman, Dave Godfrey, Keith Maillard and his advanced novel class, Barb Nickel, Zsuzsie Gardner, Sara Bershtel, Louise Dennys, and especially Riva Hocherman and Denise Bukowski.

CONTENTS

TRAPLINES

Dad takes the white marten from the trap.

"Look at that, Will," he says.

It is limp in his hands. It hasn't been dead that long.

We tramp through the snow to the end of our trapline. Dad whistles. The goner marten is over his shoulder. From here, it looks like Dad is wearing it. There is nothing else in the other traps. We head back to the truck. The snow crunches. This is the best time for trapping, Dad told me a while ago. This is when the animals are hungry.

Our truck rests by the roadside at an angle. Dad rolls the white marten in a gray canvas cover separate from the others. The marten is flawless, which is rare in these parts. I put my animals beside his and cover them. We get in the truck. Dad turns the radio on and country twang fills the cab. We smell like sweat and oil and pine. Dad hums. I stare out the window. Mrs. Smythe would say the trees here are like the ones on Christmas postcards, tall and heavy with snow. They crowd close to the road. When the wind blows strong enough, the older trees snap and fall on the power lines.

"Well, there's our Christmas money," Dad says, snatching a peek at the rearview mirror.

I look back. The wind ruffles the canvases that cover the martens. Dad is smiling. He sits back, steering with one hand. He doesn't even mind when we are passed by three cars. The lines in his face are loose now. He sings along with a woman who left her husband—even that doesn't make him mad. We have our Christmas money. At least for now, there'll be no shouting in the house. It will take Mom and Dad a few days to find something else to fight about.

The drive home is a long one. Dad changes the radio station twice. I search my brain for something to say but my headache is spreading and I don't feel like talking. He watches the road, though he keeps stealing looks at the back of the truck. I watch the trees and the cars passing us.

One of the cars has two women in it. The woman that isn't driving waves her hands around as she talks. She reminds me of Mrs. Smythe. They are beside us, then ahead of us, then gone.

Tucca is still as we drive into it. The snow drugs it, makes it lazy. Houses puff cedar smoke and the sweet, sharp smell gets in everyone's clothes. At school in town, I can close my eyes and tell who's from the village and who isn't just by smelling them.

When we get home, we go straight to the basement. Dad gives me the ratty martens and keeps the good ones. He made me start on squirrels when I was in grade five. He put the knife in my hand, saying, "For Christ's sake, it's just a squirrel. It's dead, you stupid knucklehead. It can't feel anything."

He made the first cut for me. I swallowed, closed my eyes, and lifted the knife.

"Jesus," Dad muttered. "Are you a sissy? I got a sissy for a son. Look. It's just like cutting up a chicken. See? Pretend you're skinning a chicken."

Dad showed me, then put another squirrel in front of me, and we didn't leave the basement until I got it right.

Now Dad is skinning the flawless white marten, using his best knife. His tongue is sticking out the corner of his mouth. He straightens up and shakes his skinning hand. I quickly start on the next marten. It's perfect except for a scar across its back. It was probably in a fight. We won't get much for the skin. Dad goes back to work. I stop, clench, unclench my hands. They are stiff.

"Goddamn," Dad says quietly. I look up, tensing, but Dad starts to smile. He's finished the marten. It's ready to be dried and sold. I've finished mine too. I look at my hands. They know what to do now without my having to tell them. Dad sings as we go up the creaking stairs. When we get into the hallway I breathe in, smelling fresh baked bread.

Mom is sprawled in front of the TV. Her apron is smudged with flour and she is licking her fingers. When she sees us, she stops and puts her hands in her apron pockets.

"Well?" she says.

Dad grabs her at the waist and whirls her around the living room.

"Greg! Stop it!" she says, laughing.

Flour gets on Dad and cedar chips get on Mom. They talk and I leave, sneaking into the kitchen. I swallow three aspirins for my headache, snatch two buns, and go to my room. I stop in the doorway. Eric is there, plugged into his electric guitar. He looks at the buns and pulls out an earphone.

"Give me one," he says.

I throw him the smaller bun, and he finishes it in three bites.

"The other one," he says.

I give him the finger and sit on my bed. I see him thinking about tackling me, but he shrugs and plugs himself back in. I chew on the bun, roll bits of it around in my mouth. It's still warm, and I wish I had some honey for it or some blueberry jam.

Eric leaves and comes back with six buns. He wolfs them down, cramming them into his mouth. I stick my fingers in my ears and glare at him. He can't hear himself eat. He notices me and grins. Opens his mouth so I can see. I pull out a mag and turn the pages.

Dad comes in. Eric's jaw clenches. I go into the kitchen, grabbing another bun. Mom smacks my hand. We hear Eric and Dad starting to yell. Mom rolls her eyes and puts three more loaves in the oven.

"Back later," I say.

She nods, frowning at her hands.

I walk. Think about going to Billy's house. He is seeing Elaine, though, and is getting weird. He wrote her a poem yesterday. He couldn't find anything nice to rhyme with "Elaine" so he didn't finish it.

"Pain," Craig said. "Elaine, you pain."

"Plain Elaine," Tony said.

Billy smacked Tony and they went at it in the snow. Billy gave him a face wash. That ended it, and we let Billy sit on the steps and write in peace.

"Elaine in the rain," I say. "Elaine, a flame. Cranes. Danes. Trains. My main Elaine." I kick at the slush on the ground. Billy is on his own.

I let my feet take me down the street. It starts to snow, tiny ladybug flakes. It is only four but already getting dark. Streetlights flicker on. No one but me is out walking. Snot in my nose freezes. The air is starting to burn my throat. I turn and head home. Eric and Dad should be tired by now.

Another postcard picture. The houses lining the street look snug. I hunch into my jacket. In a few weeks, Christmas lights will go up all over the village. Dad will put ours up two weeks before Christmas. We use the same set every year. We'll get a tree a week later. Mom'll decorate it. On Christmas Eve, she'll put our presents under it. Some of the presents will be wrapped in aluminum because she never buys enough wrapping paper. We'll eat turkey. Mom and Dad will go to a lot of parties and get really drunk. Eric will go to a lot of parties and get really stoned. Maybe this year I will too. Anything would be better than sitting around with Tony and Craig, listening to them gripe.

I stamp the snow off my sneakers and jeans. I open the door quietly. The TV is on loud. I can tell that it's a hockey game by the announcer's voice. I take off my shoes and jacket. The house feels really hot to me after being outside. My face starts to tingle as the skin thaws. I go into the kitchen and take another aspirin.

The kitchen could use some plants. It gets good light in the winter. Mrs. Smythe has filled her kitchen with plants, hanging the ferns by the window where the cats can't eat them. The Smythes have pictures all over their walls of places they have been—Europe, Africa, Australia. They've been everywhere. They can afford it, she says, because they don't have kids. They had one, a while ago. On the TV there's a wallet-sized picture of a dark-haired boy with his front teeth missing. He was their kid but he disappeared. Mrs. Smythe fiddles with the picture a lot.

Eric tries to sneak up behind me. His socks make a slithering sound on the floor. I duck just in time and hit him in the stomach.

He doubles over. He has a towel stretched between his hands. His choking game. He punches at me, but I hop out of the way. His fist hits the hot stove. Yelling, he jerks his hand back. I race out of the kitchen and down to the basement. Eric follows me, screaming my name. "Come out, you chicken," he says. "Come on out and fight."

I keep still behind a stack of plywood. Eric has the towel ready. After a while, he goes back upstairs and locks the door behind him.

I stand. I can't hear Mom and Dad. They must have gone out to celebrate the big catch. They'll probably find a party and go on a bender until Monday, when Dad has to go back to work. I'm alone with Eric, but he'll leave the house around ten. I can stay out of his way until then.

The basement door bursts open. I scramble under Dad's tool table. Eric must be stoned. He's probably been toking up since Mom and Dad left. Pot always makes him mean. He laughs. "You baby. You fucking baby." He doesn't look for me that hard. He thumps loudly up the stairs, slams the door shut, then tiptoes back down and waits. He must think I'm really stupid.

We stay like this for a long time. Eric lights up. In a few minutes, the whole basement smells like pot. Dad will be pissed off if the smoke ruins the white marten. I smile, hoping it does. Eric will really get it then.

"Fuck," he says and disappears upstairs, not locking the door. I crawl out. My legs are stiff. The pot is making me dizzy.

The woodstove is cooling. I don't open it because the hinges squeal. It'll be freezing down here soon. Breathing fast, I climb the stairs. I crack the door open. There are no lights on except in our bedroom. I pull on my jacket and sneakers. I grab some bread and stuff it in my jacket, then run for the door but Eric is blocking it, leering.

"Thought you were sneaky, hey," he says.

I back into the kitchen. He follows. I wait until he is near before I bend over and ram him. He's slow because of the pot and slips to the floor. He grabs my ankle, but I kick him in the head and am out the door before he can catch me. I take the steps two at a time. Eric stands on the porch and laughs. I can't wait until I'm bigger. I'd like to smear him against a wall. Let him see what it feels like. I'd like to smear him so bad.

I munch on some bread as I head for the exit to the highway. Now the snow is coming down in thick, large flakes that melt when they touch my skin. I stand at the exit and wait.

I hear One Eye's beat-up Ford long before I see it. It clunks down the road and stalls when One Eye stops for me. "You again. What you doing out here?" he yells at me.

"Waiting for Princess fucking Di," I say.

"Smart mouth. You keep it up and you can stay out there."

The back door opens anyway. Snooker and Jim are there. One Eye and Don Wilson are in the front. They all have silver lunch buckets at their feet.

We get into town and I say, "Could you drop me off here?"

One Eye looks back, surprised. He has forgotten about me. He frowns. "Where you going this time of night?"

"Disneyland," I say.

"Smart mouth," he says. "Don't be like your brother. You stay out of trouble."

I laugh. One Eye slows the car and pulls over. It chokes and sputters. I get out and thank him for the ride. One Eye grunts. He pulls away and I walk to Mrs. Smythe's.

The first time I saw her house was last spring, when she invited the English class there for a barbecue. The lawn was neat and green and I only saw one dandelion. There were rose bushes in the front and raspberry bushes in the back. I went with Tony and Craig, who got high on the way there. Mrs. Smythe noticed right away. She took them aside and talked to them. They stayed in the poolroom downstairs until the high wore off.

There weren't any other kids from the village there. Only townies. Kids that Dad says will never dirty their pink hands. They were split into little groups. They talked and ate and laughed and I wandered around alone, feeling like a dork. I was going to go downstairs to Tony and Craig when Mrs. Smythe came up to me, carrying a hot dog. I never noticed her smile until then. Her blue sundress swayed as she walked.

"You weren't in class yesterday," she said.

"Stomachache."

"I was going to tell you how much I liked your essay. You must have done a lot of work on it."

"Yeah." I tried to remember what I had written.

"Which part was the hardest?" she said.

I cleared my throat. "Starting it."

"I walked right into that one," she said, laughing. I smiled. A tall man came up and hugged her. She kissed him. "Sam," she said. "This is the student I was telling you about."

"Well, hello," Mr. Smythe said. "Great paper."

"Thanks," I said.

"Is it William or Will?" Mr. Smythe said.

"Will," I said. He held out his hand and shook mine.

"That big, huh?" he said.

Oh no, I thought, remembering what I'd written. Dad, Eric, Grandpa, and I had gone out halibut fishing once and caught a huge one. It took forever to get it in the boat and we all took turns clubbing it. But it wouldn't die, so Dad shot it. In the essay I said it was seven hundred pounds, but Mrs. Smythe had pointed out to the whole class that halibut didn't get much bigger than five hundred. Tony and Craig bugged me about that.

"Karen tells me you've written a lot about fishing," Mr. Smythe said, sounding really cheerful.

"Excuse me," Mrs. Smythe said. "That's my cue to leave. If you're smart, you'll do the same. Once you get Sam going with his stupid fish stories you can't get a word—"

Mr. Smythe goosed her. She poked him with her hot dog and left quickly. Mr. Smythe put his arm around my shoulder, shaking his head. We sat out on the patio and he told me about the time he caught a marlin and about scuba diving on the Great Barrier Reef. He went down in a shark cage once to try to film a great white eating. I told him about Uncle Bernie's gillnetter. He wanted to know if Uncle Bernie would take him out, and what gear he was going to need. We ended up in the kitchen, me using a flounder to show him how to clean a halibut.

I finally looked at the clock around eleven. Dad had said he would pick me and Tony and Craig up around eight. I didn't even know where Tony and Craig were anymore. I couldn't believe it had gotten so late without my noticing. Mrs. Smythe had gone to bed. Mr. Smythe said he would drive me home. I said that was okay, I'd hitch.

He snorted. "Karen would kill me. No, I'll drive you. Let's phone your parents and tell them you're coming home."

No one answered the phone. I said they were probably asleep. He dialed again. Still no answer.

"Looks like you've got the spare bedroom tonight," he said.

"Let me try," I said, picking up the phone. There was no answer, but after six rings I pretended Dad was on the other end. I didn't want to spend the night at my English teacher's house. Tony and Craig would never shut up about it.

"Hi, Dad," I said. "How come? I see. Car trouble. No problem. Mr. Smythe is going to drive me home. What? Sure, I—"

"Let me talk to him," Mr. Smythe said, snatching the phone. "Hello! Mr. Tate! How are you? My, my, my. Your son is a lousy liar, isn't he?" He hung up. "It's amazing how much your father sounds like a dial tone."

I picked up the phone again. "They're sleeping, that's all." Mr. Smythe watched me as I dialed. There wasn't any answer.

"Why'd you lie?" he said quietly.

We were alone in the kitchen. I swallowed. He was a lot bigger than me. When he reached over, I put my hands up and covered my face. He stopped, then took the phone out of my hands.

"It's okay," he said. "I won't hurt you. It's okay."

I put my hands down. He looked sad. That annoyed me. I shrugged, backing away. "I'll hitch," I said.

Mr. Smythe shook his head. "No, really, Karen would kill me, then she'd go after you. Come on. We'll be safer if you sleep in the spare room."

In the morning Mr. Smythe was up before I could sneak out. He was making bacon and pancakes. He asked if I'd ever done any freshwater fishing. I said no. He started talking about fishing in the Black Sea and I listened to him. He's a good cook.

Mrs. Smythe came into the kitchen dressed in some sweats and a T-shirt. She ate without saying anything and didn't look awake until she finished her coffee. Mr. Smythe phoned my house but no one answered. He asked if I wanted to go up to Old Timer's Lake with them. He had a new Sona reel he wanted to try out. I didn't have anything better to do.

The Smythes have a twenty-foot speedboat. They let me drive it around the lake a few times while Mrs. Smythe baked in the sun and Mr. Smythe put the rod together. We lazed around the beach in the afternoon, watching the people go by. Sipping their beers, the Smythes argued about who was going to drive back. We rode around the lake some more and roasted hot dogs for dinner.

Their porch light is on. I go up the walk and ring the bell. Mrs. Smythe said just come in, don't bother knocking, but I can't do that. It doesn't feel right. She opens the door, smiling when she sees me. She is wearing a fluffy pink sweater. "Hi, Will. Sam was hoping you'd drop by. He says he's looking forward to beating you."

"Dream on," I say.

She laughs. "Go right in." She heads down the hall to the washroom.

I go into the living room. Mr. Smythe isn't there. The TV is on, some documentary about whales.

He's in the kitchen, scrunched over a game of solitaire. His new glasses are sliding off his nose and he looks more like a teacher than Mrs. Smythe. He scratches the beard he's trying to grow.

"Come on in," he says, patting the chair beside him.

I take a seat and watch him finish the game. He pushes his glasses up. "What's your pleasure?" he says.

"Pool," I say.

"Feeling lucky, huh?" We go down to the poolroom. "How about a little extra this week?" he says, not looking at me.

I shrug. "Sure. Dishes?"

He shakes his head. "Bigger."

"I'm not shoveling the walk," I say.

He shakes his head again. "Bigger."

"Money?"

"Bigger."

"What?"

He racks up the balls. Sets the cue ball. Wipes his hands on his jeans.

"What?" I say again.

Mr. Smythe takes out a quarter. "Heads or tails?" he says, tossing it.

"Heads," I say.

He slaps the quarter on the back of his hand. "I break."

"Where? Let me see that," I say, laughing. He holds it up. The quarter is tails.

He breaks. "How'd you like to stay with us?" he says, very quietly.

"Sure," I say. "But I got to go back on Tuesday. We got to check the traplines again."

He is quiet. The balls make thunking sounds as they bounce around the table. "Do you like it here?"

"Sure," I say.

"Enough to live here?"

I'm not sure I heard him right. Maybe he's asking a different question from the one I think he's asking. I open my mouth. I don't know what to say. I say nothing.

"Those are the stakes, then," he says. "I win, you stay. You win, you stay."

He's joking. I laugh. He doesn't laugh. "You serious?" I ask.

He stands up straight. "I don't think I've ever been more serious."

The room is suddenly very small.

"Your turn," he says. "Stripes."

I scratch, missing the ball by a mile. He takes his turn.

"We don't want to push you," he says. He leans over the table, squints at a ball. "We just think that you'd be safer here. Hell, you practically live with us already." I watch my sneakers. He keeps playing. "We aren't rich. We aren't perfect. We . . ." He looks at me. "We thought maybe you'd like to try it for a couple of weeks first."

"I can't."

"You don't have to decide right now," he says. "Think about it. Take a few days."

It's my turn again but I don't feel like playing anymore. Mr. Smythe is waiting, though. I pick a ball. Aim, shoot, miss.

The game goes on in silence. Mr. Smythe wins easily. He smiles. "Well, I win. You stay."

If I wanted to get out of the room, there is only one door and Mr. Smythe is blocking it. He watches me. "Let's go upstairs," he says.

Mrs. Smythe has shut off the TV. She stands up when we come into the living room. "Will—"

"I asked him already," Mr. Smythe says.

Her head snaps around. "You what?"

"I asked him."

Her hands clench at her sides. "We were supposed to do it together, Sam." Her voice is flat. She turns to me. "You said no."

I can't look at her. I look at the walls, at the floor, at her slippers. I shouldn't have come tonight. I should have waited for Eric to leave. She stands in front of me, trying to smile. Her hands are warm on my face. "Look at me," she says. "Will? Look at me." She is trying to smile. "Hungry?" she says.

I nod. She makes a motion with her head for Mr. Smythe to follow her into the kitchen. When they're gone I sit down. It should be easy. It should be easy. I watch TV without seeing it. I wonder what they're saying about me in the kitchen.

It's now almost seven and my ribs hurt. Mostly, I can ignore it, but Eric hit me pretty hard and they're bruised. Eric got hit pretty hard by Dad, so we're even, I guess. I'm counting the days until Eric moves out. The rate he's going, he'll be busted soon anyway. Tony says the police are starting to ask questions.

It's a strange night. We all pretend that nothing has happened and Mrs. Smythe fixes some nachos. Mr. Smythe gets out a pack of Uno cards and we play a few rounds and watch the Discovery Channel. We go to bed.

I lie awake. My room. This could be my room. I already have most of my books here. It's hard to study with Eric around. I still have a headache. I couldn't get away from them long enough to sneak into the kitchen for an aspirin. I pull my T-shirt up and take a look. There's a long bruise under my ribs and five smaller ones above it. I think Eric was trying to hit my stomach but he was so wasted he kept missing. It isn't too bad. Tony's dad broke three of his ribs once. Billy got a concussion a couple of weeks ago. My dad is pretty easy. It's only Eric who really bothers me.

The Smythes keep the aspirin by the spices. I grab six, three for now and three for the morning. I'm swallowing the last one when Mr. Smythe grabs my hand. I didn't even hear him come in. I must be sleepy.

"Where'd they hit you this time?" he says.

"I got a headache," I say. "A bad one."

He pries open the hand with the aspirins in it. "How many do you plan on taking?"

"These are for later."

He sighs. I get ready for a lecture. "Go back to bed" is all he says. "It'll be okay." He sounds very tired.

"Sure," I say.

I get up around five. I leave a note saying I have things to do at home. I catch a ride with some guys coming off the graveyard shift.

No one is home. Eric had a party last night. I'm glad I wasn't around. They've wrecked the coffee table and the rug smells like stale beer and cigarettes. Our bedroom is even worse. Someone puked all over Eric's bed and there are two used condoms on mine. At least none of the windows were broken this time. I start to clean my side of the room, then stop. I sit on my bed.

Mr. Smythe will be getting up soon. It's Sunday, so there'll be waffles or french toast. He'll fix a plate of bacon and eat it before Mrs. Smythe comes downstairs. He thinks she doesn't know that he does this. She'll get up around ten or eleven and won't talk to anyone until she's had about three coffees. She starts to wake up around one or two. They'll argue about something. Whose turn to take out the garbage or do the laundry. They'll read the paper.

I crawl into bed. The aspirin isn't working. I try to sleep but it really reeks in here. I have a biology test tomorrow. I forgot to bring the book back from their place. I lie there awake until our truck pulls into the driveway. Mom and Dad are fighting. They sound plastered. Mom is bitching about something. Dad is not saying anything. Doors slam.

Mom comes in first and goes straight to bed. She doesn't seem to notice the house is a mess. Dad comes in a lot slower.

"What the—Eric!" he yells. "Eric!"

I pretend to sleep. The door bangs open.

"Eric, you little bastard," Dad says, looking around. He shakes me. "Where the fuck is Eric?"

His breath is lethal. You can tell he likes his rye straight.

"How should I know?"

He rips Eric's amplifiers off the walls. He throws them down and gives them a good kick. He tips Eric's bed over. Eric is smart. He won't come home for a while. Dad will have cooled off by then and Eric can give him some money without Dad's getting pissed off. I don't move. I wait until he's out of the room before I put on a sweater. I can hear him down in the basement chopping wood. It should be around eight by now. The RinkyDink will be open in an hour.

When I go into the kitchen, Mom is there. She sees me and makes a shushing motion with her hands. She pulls out a bottle from behind the stove and sits down at the kitchen table.

"You're a good boy," she says, giggling. "You're a good boy. Help your old mother back to bed, hey."

"Sure," I say, putting an arm around her. She stands, holding onto the bottle with one hand and me with the other. "This way, my lady."

"You making fun of me?" she says, her eyes going small. "You laughing at me?" Then she laughs and we go to their room. She flops onto the bed. She takes a long drink. "You're fucking laughing at me, aren't you?"

"Mom, you're paranoid. I was making a joke."

"Yeah, you're really funny. A laugh a minute," she says, giggling again. "Real comedian."

"Yeah, that's me."

She throws the bottle at me. I duck. She rolls over and starts to cry. I cover her with the blanket and leave. The floor is sticky. Dad's still chopping wood. They wouldn't notice if I wasn't here. Maybe people would talk for a week or two, but after a while they wouldn't notice. The only people who would miss me are Tony and Craig and Billy and maybe Eric, when he got toked up and didn't have anything for target practice.

Billy is playing Mortal Kombat at the RinkyDink. He's chain-smoking. As I walk up to him, he turns around quickly.

"Oh, it's you," he says, going back to the game.

"Hi to you too," I say.

"You seen Elaine?" he says.

"Nope."

He crushes out his cigarette in the ashtray beside him. He plays for a while, loses a life, then shakes another cigarette out one-handed. He sticks it in his mouth, loses another man, then lights up. He sucks deep. "Relax," I say. "Her majesty's limo is probably stuck in traffic. She'll come."

He glares at me. "Shut up."

I go play pool with Craig, who's decided that he's James Dean. He's wearing a white T-shirt, jeans, and a black leather jacket that looks like his brother's. His hair is blow-dried and a cigarette dangles from the corner of his mouth.

"What a loser," he says.

"Who you calling a loser?"

"Billy. What a loser." He struts to the other side of the pool table.

"He's okay."

"That babe," he says. "What's-her-face. Ellen? Irma?"

"Elaine."

"Yeah, her. She's going out with him 'cause she's got a bet."

"What?"

"She's got to go out with him a month, and her friend will give her some coke."

"Billy's already giving her coke."

"Yeah. He's a loser."

I look over at Billy. He's lighting another cigarette.

"Can you imagine a townie wanting anything to do with him?" Craig says. "She's just doing it as a joke. She's going to dump him in a week. She's going to put all his stupid poems in the paper."

I see it now. There's a space around Billy. No one is going near him. He doesn't notice. Same with me. I catch some guys I used to hang out with grinning at me. When they see me looking at them, they look away.

Craig wins the game. I'm losing a lot this week.

Elaine gets to the RinkyDink after lunch. She's got some townie girlfriends with her who are tiptoeing around like they're going to get jumped. Elaine leads them right up to Billy. Everyone's watching. Billy gives her his latest poem. I wonder what he found to rhyme with "Elaine."

The girls leave. Billy holds the door open for Elaine. Her friends start to giggle. The guys standing around start to howl. They're laughing so hard they're crying. I feel sick. I think about telling Billy but I know he won't listen.

I leave the RinkyDink and go for a walk. I walk and walk and end up back in front of the RinkyDink. There's nowhere else to go. I hang out with Craig, who hasn't left the pool table.

I spend the night on his floor. Craig's parents are Jehovah's Witnesses and preach at me before I go to bed. I sit and listen because I need a place to sleep. I'm not going home until tomorrow, when Mom and Dad are sober. Craig's mom gets us up two hours before the bus that takes the village kids to school comes. They pray before we eat. Craig looks at me and rolls his eyes. People are always making fun of Craig because his parents stand on the corner downtown every Friday and hold up the *Watchtower* mags. When his parents start to bug him, he says he'll take up devil worship or astrology if they don't lay off. I think I'll ask him if he wants to hang out with me on Christmas. His parents don't believe in it.

Between classes I pass Mrs. Smythe in the hall. Craig nudges me. "Go on," he says, making sucking noises. "Go get your A."

"Fuck off," I say, pushing him.

She's talking to some girl and doesn't see me. I think about skipping English but know that she'll call home and ask where I am.

At lunch no one talks to me. I can't find Craig or Tony or Billy. The village guys who hang out by the science wing snicker as I go past. I don't stop until I get to the gym doors, where the headbangers have taken over. I don't have any money and I didn't bring a lunch, so I bum a cigarette off this girl with really tight jeans. To get my mind off my stomach I try to get her to go out with me. She looks at me like I'm crazy. When she walks away, the fringe on her leather jacket swings.

I flunk my biology test. It's multiple choice. I stare at the paper and kick myself. I know I could have passed if I'd read the chapter. Mr. Kellerman reads out the scores from lowest to highest. My name is called out third.

"Mr. Tate," he says. "Three out of thirty."

"All riiight," Craig says, slapping my back.

"Mr. Davis," Mr. Kellerman says to Craig, "three and a half."

Craig stands up and bows. The guys in the back clap. The kids in the front laugh. Mr. Kellerman reads out the rest of the scores. Craig turns to me. "Looks like I beat the Brain," he says.

"Yeah," I say. "Pretty soon you're going to be getting the Nobel Prize."

The bell rings for English. I go to my locker and take out my jacket. If she calls home no one's going to answer anyway.

I walk downtown. The snow is starting to slack off and it's
even sunning a bit. My stomach growls. I haven't eaten anything since breakfast. I wish I'd gone to English. Mrs. Smythe
would have given me something to eat. She always has something left over from lunch. I hunch down into my jacket.

Downtown, I go to the Paradise Arcade. All the heads
hang out there. Maybe Eric'll give me some money. More
like a belt, but it's worth a try. I don't see him anywhere,
though. In fact, no one much is there. Just some burnouts by
the pinball machines. I see Mitch and go over to him, but he's
soaring, laughing at the ball going around the machine. I walk
away, head for the highway, and hitch home. Mom will have
passed out by now, and Dad'll be at work.

Sure enough, Mom is on the living room floor. I get her a
blanket. The stove has gone out and it's freezing in here. I
go into the kitchen and look through the fridge. There's one
jar of pickles, some really pathetic-looking celery, and some
milk that's so old it smells like cheese. There's no bread left
over from Saturday. I find some Rice-A-Roni and cook it.
Mom comes to and asks for some water. I bring her a glass
and give her a little Rice-A-Roni. She makes a face but slowly
eats it.

At six Dad comes home with Eric. They've made up. Eric
has bought Dad a six-pack and they watch the hockey game
together. I stay in my room. Eric has cleaned his bed by
dumping his mattress outside and stealing mine. I haul my
mattress back onto my bed frame. I pull out my English
book. We have a grammar test this Friday. I know Mrs.
Smythe will be unhappy if she has to fail me. I read the chap-

ter on nouns and get through most of the one on verbs before Eric comes in and kicks me off the bed.

He tries to take the mattress but I punch him in the side. Eric turns and grabs my hair. "This is my bed," he says. "Understand?"

"Fuck you," I say. "You had the party. Your fucked-up friends trashed the room. You sleep on the floor."

Dad comes in and sees Eric push me against the wall and smack my face. He yells at Eric, who turns around, his fist frozen in the air. Dad rolls his sleeves up.

"You always take his side!" Eric yells. "You never take mine!"

"Pick on someone your own size," Dad says. "Unless you want to deal with me."

Eric gives me a look that says he'll settle with me later. I pick up my English book and get out. I walk around the village, staying away from the RinkyDink. It's the first place Eric will look.

I'm at the village exit. The sky is clear and the stars are popping out. Mr. Smythe will be at his telescope trying to map the Pleiades. Mrs. Smythe will be marking papers while she watches TV.

"Need a ride?" this guy says. There's a blue pickup stopped in front of me. The driver is wearing a hunting cap.

I take my hand out of my mouth. I've been chewing my knuckle like a baby. I shake my head. "I'm waiting for someone," I say.

He shrugs and takes off. I stand there and watch his headlights disappear.

They didn't really mean it. They'd get bored of me quick

when they found out what I'm like. I should have just said yes. I could have stayed until they got fed up and then come home when Eric had cooled off.

Two cars pass me as I walk back to the village. I can hide at Tony's until Eric goes out with his friends and forgets this afternoon. My feet are frozen by the time I get to the RinkyDink. Tony is there.

"So. I heard Craig beat you in biology," he says.

I laugh. "Didn't it just impress you?"

"A whole half a point. Way to go," he says. "For a while there we thought you were getting townie."

"Yeah, right," I say. "Listen, I pissed Eric off—"

"Surprise, surprise."

"—and I need a place to crash. Can I sleep over?"

"Sure," he says. Mitch wanders into the RinkyDink, and a crowd of kids slowly drifts over to him. He looks around, eyeing everybody. Then he starts giving something out. Me and Tony go over.

"Wow," Tony says, after Mitch gives him something too. "What?"

We leave and go behind the RinkyDink, where other kids are gathered. "Fucking all right," I hear Craig say, even though I can't see him.

"What?" I say. Tony opens his hand. He's holding a little vial with white crystals in it.

"Crack," he says. "Man, is he stupid. He could have made a fortune and he's just giving it away."

We don't have a pipe, and Tony wants to do this right the first time. He decides to save it for tomorrow, after he buys the right equipment. I'm hungry again. I'm about to tell him that I'm going to Billy's when I see Eric.

"Shit," I say and hide behind him.

Tony looks up. "Someone's in trou-ble," he sings.

Eric's looking for me. I hunch down behind Tony, who tries to look innocent. Eric spots him and starts to come over. "Better run," Tony whispers.

I sneak behind some other people but Eric sees me and I have to run for it anyway. Tony starts to cheer and the kids behind the RinkyDink join in. Some of the guys follow us so they'll see what happens when Eric catches up with me. I don't want to find out so I pump as hard as I can.

Eric used to be fast. I'm glad he's a dopehead now because he can't really run anymore. I'm panting and my legs are cramping but the house is in sight. I run up the stairs. The door is locked.

I stand there, hand on the knob. Eric rounds the corner to our block. There's no one behind him. I bang on the door but now I see that our truck is gone. I run around to the back but the basement door is locked too. Even the windows are locked.

Eric pops his head around the corner of the house. He grins when he sees me, then disappears. I grit my teeth and start running across our backyard. Head for Billy's. "You shithead," Eric yells. He has a friend with him, maybe Brent. I duck behind our neighbor's house. There's snow in my sneakers and all the way up my leg, but I'm sweating. I stop. I can't hear Eric. I hope I've lost him, but Eric is really pissed off and when he's pissed off he doesn't let go. I look down.

My footprints are clear in the snow. I start to run again, but I hit a thick spot and have to wade through thigh-high snow. I look back. Eric is nowhere. I keep slogging. I make it to the road again and run down to the exit.

I've lost him. I'm shaking because it's cold. I can feel the sweat cooling on my skin. My breath goes back to normal. I wait for a car to come by. I've missed the night shift and the graveyard crew won't be by until midnight. It's too cold to wait that long.

A car, a red car. A little Toyota. Brent's car. I run off the road and head for a clump of trees. The Toyota pulls over and Eric gets out, yelling. I reach the trees and rest. They're waiting by the roadside. Eric is peering into the trees, trying to see me. Brent is smoking in the car. Eric crosses his arms over his chest and blows into his hands. My legs are frozen.

After a long time, a cop car cruises to a stop beside the Toyota. I wade out and wave at the two policemen. They look startled. One of them turns to Eric and Brent and asks them something. I see Eric shrug. It takes me a while to get over to where they're standing because my legs are slow.

The cop is watching me. I swear I'll never call them pigs again. I swear it. He leans over to Brent, who digs around in the glove compartment. The cop says something to his partner. I scramble down the embankment.

Eric has no marks on his face. Dad probably hit him on the back and stomach. Dad has been careful since the social worker came to our house. Eric suddenly smiles at me and holds out his hand. I move behind the police car.

"Is there a problem here?" the policeman says.

"No," Eric says. "No probulum. Li'l misunnerstanin'."

Oh, shit. He's as high as a kite. The policeman looks hard at Eric. I look at the car. Brent is staring at me, glassy-eyed. He's high too.

Eric tries again to reach out to me. I put the police car between us. The policeman grabs Eric by the arm and his partner goes and gets Brent. The policeman says something about driving under the influence but none of us are listening. Eric's eyes are on me. I'm going to pay for this. Brent is swearing. He wants a lawyer. He stumbles out of the Toyota and slips on the road. Brent and Eric are put in the backseat of the police car. The policeman comes up to me and says, "Can you make it home?"

I nod.

"Good. Go," he says.

They drive away. When I get home, I walk around the house, trying to figure out a way to break in. I find a stick and jimmy the basement door open. Just in case Eric gets out tonight, I make a bed under the tool table and go to sleep.

No one is home when I wake up. I scramble an egg and get ready for school. I sit beside Tony on the bus.

"I was expecting to see you with black eyes," he says.

My legs are still raw from last night. I have something due today but I can't remember what. If Eric is in the drunk tank, they'll let him out later.

The village guys are talking to me again. I skip gym. I skip history. I hang out with Craig and Tony in the Paradise Arcade. I'm not sure if I want to be friends with them after they joined in the chase last night, but it's better to have them on my side than not. They get a two-for-one pizza special for lunch and I'm glad I stuck with them because I'm starved. They also got some five-finger specials from Safeway. Tony is proud because he swiped a couple of bags of chips and two Pepsis and no one even noticed.

Mitch comes over to me in the bathroom.

"That was a really cheap thing to do," he says.

"What?" I haven't done anything to him.

"What? What? Getting your brother thrown in jail. Pretty crummy."

"He got himself thrown in jail. He got caught when he was high."

"That's not what he says." Mitch frowns. "He says you set him up."

"Fuck." I try to sound calm. "When'd he tell you that?"

"This morning," he says. "He's waiting for you at school."

"I didn't set him up. How could I?"

Mitch nods. He hands me some crack and says, "Hey, I'm sorry," and leaves. I look at it. I'll give it to Tony and maybe he'll let me stay with him tonight.

Billy comes into the Paradise with Elaine and her friends. He's getting some glances but he doesn't notice. He holds the chair out for Elaine, who sits down without looking at him. I don't want to be around for this. I go over to Tony.

"I'm leaving," I say.

Tony shushes me. "Watch," he says.

Elaine orders a beer. Frankie shakes his head and points to the sign that says WE DO NOT SERVE MINORS. Elaine frowns. She says something to Billy. He shrugs. She orders a Coke. Billy pays. When their Cokes come, Elaine dumps hers over Billy's head. Billy stares at her, more puzzled than anything else. Her friends start to laugh, and I get up and walk out.

I lean against the wall of the Paradise. Billy comes out a few minutes later. His face is still and pale. Elaine and her friends follow him, reciting lines from the poems he wrote her. Tony and the rest spill out too, laughing. I go back inside and trade the crack for some quarters for the video games. I keep losing. Tony wants to go now and we hitch back to the village. We raid his fridge and have chocolate ice cream coconut sundaes. Angela comes in with Di and says that Eric is looking for me. I look at Tony and he looks at me.

"Boy, are you in for it," Tony says. "You'd better stay here tonight."

When everyone is asleep, Tony pulls out a weird-looking pipe and does the crack. His face goes very dreamy and far away. A few minutes later he says, "Christ, that's great. I wonder how much Mitch has?"

I turn over and go to sleep.

The next morning Billy is alone on the bus. No one wants to sit with him so there are empty seats all around him. He looks like he hasn't slept. Tony goes up to him and punches him in the arm.

"So how's Shakespeare this morning?" Tony says.

I hope Eric isn't at the school. I don't know where else I can hide.

Mrs. Smythe is waiting at the school bus stop. I sneak out the back door of the bus, with Tony and the guys pretending to fight to cover me.

We head back to the Paradise. I'm starting to smell bad. I haven't had a shower in days. I wish I had some clean clothes. I wish I had some money to buy a toothbrush. I hate the scummy feeling on my teeth. I wish I had enough for a taco or a hamburger.

Dad is at the Paradise, looking for me.

"Let's go to the Dairy Queen," he says.

He orders a coffee, a chocolate milk shake, and a cheeseburger. We take the coffee and milk shake to a back table, and I pocket the order slip. We sit there. Dad folds and unfolds a napkin.

"One of your teachers called," he says.

"Mrs. Smythe?"

"Yeah." He looks up. "Says she'd like you to stay there."

I try to read his face. His eyes are bloodshot and red-rimmed. He must have a big hangover.

The cashier calls out our number. I go up and get the cheeseburger and we split it. Dad always eats slow to make it last longer.

"Did you tell her you wanted to?"

"No," I say. "They asked me, but I said I couldn't."

Dad nods. "Did you tell them anything?"

"Like what?"

"Don't get smart," he says, sounding beat.

"I didn't say anything."

He stops chewing. "Then why'd they ask you?"

"Don't know."

"You must have told them something."

"Nope. They just asked."

"Did Eric tell them?"

I snort. "Eric? No way. They would . . . He wouldn't go anywhere near them. They're okay, Dad. They won't tell anybody."

"So you did tell them."

"I didn't. I swear I didn't. Look, Eric got me on the face a couple of times and they just figured it out."

"You're lying."

I finished my half of the cheeseburger. "I'm not lying. I didn't say anything and they won't either."

"I never touched you."

"Yeah, Eric took care of that," I say. "You seen him?"

"I kicked him out."

"You what?"

"Party. Ruined the basement," Dad says grimly. "He's old enough. Had to leave sooner or later."

He chews his last mouthful of cheeseburger. Eric will really be out of his mind now.

We drive out to check the trapline. The first trap has been tripped with a stick. Dad curses, blaming the other trappers who have lines near ours. "I'll skunk them," he says. But the last three traps have got some more martens. We even get a little lynx. Dad is happy. We go home. The basement is totally ripped apart.

Next day at school, I spend most of the time ducking from Eric and Mrs. Smythe before I finally get sick of the whole lot and go down to the Paradise. Tony is there with Billy, who asks me if I want to go to Vancouver with him until Eric cools off.

"Now?"

"No better time," he says.

I think about it. "When you leaving?"

"Tonight."

"I don't know. I don't have any money."

"Me neither," he says.

"Shit," I say. "How we going to get there? It's a zillion miles from here."

"Hitch to town, hitch to Smithers, then down to Prince George."

"Yeah, yeah, but what are we going to eat?"

He wiggles his hand. Five-finger special. I laugh.

"You change your mind," he says, "I'll be behind the RinkyDink around seven. Get some thick boots."

We're about to hitch home when I see Mrs. Smythe peer into the Paradise. It's too late to hide because she sees me. Her face stiffens. She walks over to us and the guys start to laugh. Mrs. Smythe looks at them, then at me.

"Will?" she says. "Can I talk to you outside?"

She glances around like the guys are going to jump her. I try to see what she's nervous about. Tony is grabbing his crotch. Billy is cleaning his nails. The other guys are snickering. I suddenly see them the way she does. They all have long, greasy hair, combed straight back. We're all wearing jeans, T-shirts, and sneakers. We don't look nice.

She's got on her school uniform, as she calls it. Dark skirt, white shirt, low black heels, glasses. She's watching me like she hasn't seen me before. I hope she never sees my house.

"Later?" I say. "I'm kind of busy."

She blushes, the guys laugh hard. I wish I could take the words back. "Are you sure?" she says.

Tony nudges my arm. "Why don't you introduce us to your girlfriend," he says. "Maybe she'd like—"

"Shut up," I say. Mrs. Smythe has no expression now.

"I'll talk to you later, then," she says, and turns around and walks out without looking back. If I could, I'd follow her.

Billy claps me on the shoulder. "Stay away from them," he says. "It's not worth it."

It doesn't matter. She practically said she didn't want to see me again. I don't blame her. I wouldn't want to see me again either.

She'll get into her car now and go home. She'll honk when she pulls into the driveway so Mr. Smythe will come out and help her with the groceries. She always gets groceries today. The basics and sardines. Peanut butter. I lick my lips. Diamante frozen pizzas. Oodles of Noodles. Waffles. Blueberry Mueslix.

Mr. Smythe will come out of the house, wave, come down the driveway. They'll take the groceries into the house after they kiss. They'll kick the snow off their shoes and throw something in the microwave. Watch *Cheers* reruns on Channel 8. Mr. Smythe will tell her what happened in his day. Maybe she will say happened in hers.

We catch a ride home. Billy yabbers about Christmas in Vancouver, and how great it's going to be, the two of us, no one to boss us around, no one to bother us, going anywhere we want. I turn away from him. Watch the trees blur past. I guess anything'll be better than sitting around, listening to Tony and Craig gripe.

Dogs in Winter

Aunt Genna's poodle, Picnic, greeted people by humping their legs. He had an incredible grip. A new postman once dragged Picnic six blocks. Picnic bumped and ground as they went; the postman swore and whacked at the poodle with his mailbag.

Picnic humped the wrong leg, however, when he burst out of our lilac bushes and attached himself to one of Officer Wilkenson's calves. I was lounging on the porch swing, watching hummingbirds buzz around the feeder. On that quiet, lazy summer afternoon, traffic on the nearby highway was pleasantly muted.

"Whose fucking dog is this?" A man's yell broke the silence.

I sat up. A policeman was trying to pry Picnic off his leg. Picnic was going at it steady as a jackhammer.

"Frank! Get this thing off me!" the policeman said to his partner, who was unhelpfully snapping Polaroids.

The policeman lifted his leg and shook it hard. Picnic hopped off and attacked the other leg. The officer gave Picnic a kick that would have disabled a lesser dog. Not Picnic. I brought them the broom from the porch, but not even a sharp rap with a broom handle could quell Picnic's passion.

"Oh my," Aunt Genna said, arriving on the porch with a tray of lemonade. She had rushed inside when she saw the police officers coming because she wanted to get refreshments. I didn't know it at the time, but they kept returning to ask if Mama had contacted me since her jailbreak. I just thought they really liked Aunt Genna's cookies. She was always hospitable, the very picture of a grand Victorian lady, with her hair up in a big salt-and-pepper bun on top of her head. The lace on her dress fluttered as she put the tray down and rushed to the walkway where the policemen stood.

"Is—this—your—dog?" the policeman hissed.

"Why, yes, Officer Wilkenson." She knelt to help them pry Picnic from the policeman's foot. "I'm so sorry. Are you hurt?"

"Can you just hold it for a moment?" Officer Wilkenson's partner said to Aunt Genna, holding up his Polaroid. "I want to get you all in."

There is a lake I go to in my dreams. Mama took me there when I got my period for the first time.

In the dream, she and I are sitting on the shore playing kazoos. Mama has a blue kazoo; mine is pink. We play something classical. Crickets are chirping. The sun is rising slowly over the mountains. The lake is cool and dark and flat as glass.

A moose crashes through the underbrush. It lumbers to the edge of the lake, then raises its head and bellows.

Mama puts her kazoo down quietly. She reaches behind her and pulls a shotgun from the duffle bag. She hands me the gun. We have trained for this moment. I steady the gun on my shoulder, take aim, then gently squeeze the trigger.

The sound of the shot explodes in my ear. A hole appears between the moose's eyes. I don't know what I expected, maybe the moose's head to explode like a dropped pumpkin, but not the tidy red hole. The moose collapses forward, head-first into the water.

"Let's get breakfast," Mama says.

Wearing my blue dress, I walk calmly into the lake. The pebbles on the shore are all rose quartz, round and smooth as Ping-Pong balls. As I go deeper into the lake, my dress floats up around me. When I am in up to my waist, I see the moose surfacing. It rises out of the water, its coat dripping, its eyes filled with dirt. It towers over me, whispering, mud dribbling from its mouth like saliva. I lean toward it, but no matter how hard I try, I can never understand what the moose is saying.

Paul and Janet are the parents I've always wanted. Sometimes I feel like I've stepped into a storybook or into a TV set. The day we were introduced, I don't know what the counselors had told them, but they were trying not to look apprehensive. Janet was wearing a navy dress with a white Peter Pan collar. Light makeup, pearls, white shoes. Her blond hair was bobbed and tucked behind her ears. She looked like the elementary school teacher that she was. Paul had on stiff, clean jeans and an expensive-looking shirt.

"Hello, Lisa," Janet said, tentatively holding out her hands.

I stayed where I was. At thirteen, I felt gawky and awkward in clothes that didn't quite fit me and weren't in fashion. Paul and Janet looked like a couple out of a Disney movie. I couldn't believe my luck. I didn't trust it. "Are you my new parents?"

Janet nodded.

We went to McDonald's and I had a Happy Meal. It was my first time at a McDonald's. Mama didn't like restaurants of any kind. The Happy Meal came with a free toy—a plastic Garfield riding a motor scooter. I still have it on my bookshelf.

Paul and Janet talked cautiously about my new school, my room, meeting their parents. I couldn't get over how perfect they looked, how normal they seemed. I didn't want to say anything to them about Mama. If I did, they might send me back like a defective toaster.

The first time I saw Aunt Genna, the sun was high and blinding. She came out to the porch with lemonade and told her poodle Picnic to leave me alone. Picnic jumped up on me, licking my face when I bent to pet her. I ran across the yard, squealing and half afraid, half delighted. Aunt Genna tucked her dogs up with quilts embroidered with their names. She served them breakfast and dinner on porcelain plates. Aunt Genna took me in when Mama went to jail that first time, took me in like another stray dog, embroidered my pillow with my name, served me lemonade and cookies in miniature tea sets. One of her dogs—Jenjen, Coco, or Picnic—was always following her. Although she was born in Bended River, Manitoba, she liked to believe she was an English lady.

We had tea parties every Sunday after church. Aunt Genna brought out her plastic dishes and sat the dogs on cushions. Jenjen and Coco loved teatime. I would serve them doggie biscuits from plates decorated with blue bears and red balloons. Picnic didn't like to sit at the table and would whine until Aunt Genna let him go to his hall-way chair.

Since I wasn't allowed to have real tea, Aunt Genna filled the silver teapot with grape juice.

"How are you today, Lady Lisa?" she would ask, in her best English accent.

"Oh, I am quite fine," I would say. "And yourself?"

"Quite well, except that I have gout."

"Oh, how awful! Is it very painful?"

"It makes my nose itchy."

"Would you like a scone?"

"I'd adore one."

It was at one of these tea parties that I first asked about my parents. Jenjen was gnawing at her biscuit, spreading crumbs on the table. Coco and Picnic were howling. I poured grape juice for both of us, then said, "Are my parents dead?"

"No," Aunt Genna said. "They are in Africa."

I put down my cup and crawled into Aunt Genna's lap. "What are they doing in Africa?"

"They are both doctors and great explorers. They wanted so very much to take you with them, but there are too many snakes and tigers in Africa. They were afraid you'd be eaten."

"But why did they go?"

"They went because they were needed there. There are very few doctors in Africa, you see, and every single one counts."

"But why did they go?"

"Lady Lisa," Aunt Genna said, kissing the top of my head. "My Lady Lisa, they didn't want to leave you. Your mother cried and cried when they took you out of her arms. Oh, how she cried. She was so very sad."

"Then why did she go?"

"She had no choice. Duty called. She was called to Africa."

"Was my father called too?"

"Yes. Your mother took him with her. They went together."

"When are they coming back?"

"Not for a long, long time."

I put my arms around her and cried.

"But I will always be here for you," she said, patting my back. "I will always be here, my Lady Lisa."

Aunt Genna told me other things. She told me there were monsters and bogeymen in the world, but all you had to do was be a good girl and they wouldn't get you. I always believed Aunt Genna until Mama killed her.

Janet liked these wierd art movies that never made it to the Rupert theaters. She was always renting stuff with subtitles, dark lighting, talking heads, and bad special effects. This one was called *Street Angel*, and I secretly hoped it would have some sex, but when the movie opened in a squalid hut, I wondered if Janet would believe me if I said I wanted to do homework. For the first few minutes nothing happened, except this grimy, skinny kid scrounged through garbage heaps for food. In the backround there were all these dogs getting kicked and shot and run over. Then the kid was in an alley and it began to snow. I stayed very still, not really paying attention to the end, my mind stuck on the scene where this old dog collapsed and the rest of the pack circled, sniffing its body. A skinny brown mutt nipped at the old dog's leg. The dog growled deep in its throat and staggered to its feet. I knew what was coming. I knew and I couldn't stop watching. The mutt ripped into its stomach. The scene went on and on until the dog stopped yelping and jerking on the ground, its eyes flat as the mutt dragged its intestines away from the feeding frenzy. The boy kicked the pack aside and stood over the body. He picked up a cigarette butt and stuck it in the dead dog's mouth.

I saw Mama on a talk show one day.

She was hooked in from her cell via satellite. Another woman, one who had murdered her mother and her grandmother, sat in front of the studio audience, handcuffed to the chair. Next to her was a girl who had drowned her baby in a toilet, thinking it had been sent to her by the devil.

Mama wore no makeup. Her hair was pulled back and gray streaks showed through the brown. She looked wan.

Sometimes, when she gestured, I could see the belly shackle that bound her wrists to her waist.

The talk-show host gave the microphone to a man from the audience who asked, "When was the first time you killed?"

For a long time Mama said nothing. She stared straight into the camera, as if she could see the audience.

"I lost my virginity when I was twenty-seven," Mama said.

"That wasn't the question," the talk-show host said impatiently.

Mama smiled, as if they hadn't got the punch line. "I know what the question was."

I shut the TV off.

How old was I the first time I saw Mama kill? I can't remember. I was small. Not tall enough to see over our neighbor's fence. Our neighbor, Mr. Watley, built a fence to keep kids from raiding his apple orchard. It was flat cedar planks all the way round to the back, where he'd put up chicken wire. When the fence didn't keep them out, he bought a Pit Bull, a squat black-and-brown dog with bowlegs.

I had to pass Mr. Watley's house on the way home from school. I could hear the dog pacing me, panting loud. Once, I stopped by the fence to see what would happen. The dog growled long and low. The hair stood up on the back of my neck and on my arms and legs.

"Who's there?" Mr. Watley called out. "Sic 'em, Ginger."

Ginger hit the fence. It wobbled and creaked. I shrieked and ran home.

After that I walked home on the other side of the street,

but I could still hear Ginger. I could hear her when she growled. I could sense her pacing me.

None of the kids liked to play at my house. No one wanted to go near Ginger.

A carload of teenagers drove by Mr. Watley's house the morning Mama killed. They hung out the windows, and one of them came up and pounded on the fence until Ginger howled in frustration. When Mr. Watley opened his door, they threw beer bottles. He swore at them. I heard him from my bedroom. Down in the yard, Ginger kept ramming into the fence. She'd run up to it and try to jump and hit it. The fence shuddered.

"Stay away from that man," Mama said to me before I left for school. "He's crazy."

All day long at school I'd been dreading the walk home. I waited on the other side of the street, just before Mr. Watley's house. My thermos rattled in my lunch box as my hands shook.

Ginger barked.

I waited until I saw Mama peeking out the kitchen. I felt a bit safer, but not much. I ran. Maybe it was stupid, but I wanted to be inside. I wanted to be with Mama. I remember looking both ways before crossing the street, the way I'd been taught. I ran across the street with my thermos clunking against the apple that I hadn't eaten and hadn't been able to trade. Running, reaching our lawn, and thinking, I'm safe, like playing tag and getting to a safety zone where you can't be touched. I remember the sound of wood breaking and I turned.

Ginger bounded toward me and I couldn't move, I just couldn't move. She stopped two feet away and snarled and I couldn't make any muscle in my body move. Ginger's teeth were very white and her lips were pulled back way up over her gums.

I found my voice and I screamed.

The dog leapt and I banged my lunch box against the side of her head and her jaws snapped shut on my wrist. There was no pain, but I screamed again when I saw the blood. I dropped the lunch box and Ginger let go because Mama was running toward us. Mama was coming and she was shrieking.

It was as unreal then as it is now. Mama and Ginger running toward each other. They ran in slow motion, like lovers bounding across a sunlit field. Mama's arm pulled back before they met and years later I would be in art class and see a picture of a peasant woman in a field with a curved knife, a scythe, cutting wheat. Her pose, the lines of her body would be so like Mama's that I would leave the class, run down the hallway to the bathroom, and heave until I vomited.

Mama slid the knife across Ginger's scalp, lopping off the skin above her eyebrows. Ginger yelped. Mama brought her knife up and down. Ginger squealed, snapped her jaws at Mama, and crawled backward. Up and down. Mama's rapt face. Up and down. The blood making patterns on her dress like the ink blots on a Rorschach test.

The moose's short neck makes her unsuited for grazing; consequently, she is a browser. Her preference runs to willow, fir, aspen, and birch, as well as the aquatic plants found at the bottoms of lakes. The moose is quite able to defend herself;

even grizzly bears and wolf packs think twice before attempting to kill the largest member of the deer family. Much of the moose's time is spent in the water. She is an excellent swimmer, easily covering fifteen or twenty miles. She is a powerful traveler on land, too, trotting uphill or jumping fallen branches for hour after hour.

During the rutting season, her mate, the bull moose, is one of the most dangerous animals, frenzied enough to inflict death or dismemberment on those who stand between him and her and incapable of distinguishing between friend and enemy.

A man and a woman came into our backyard. The woman knelt beside me as I lay back in my lawn chair feeling the drizzle on my face. She touched my hand and said, "Your mother's been asking for you."

Her hair and skin were tinged blue by the diffused light through her umbrella. She showed me a card. I didn't bother reading it, knew just by looking at her perfectly groomed face that she was someone's hound dog.

"Janet's in the house," I said, deciding to play dense. It never worked.

Her hand squeezed my arm. "Your real mother."

I wondered what she did when she wasn't trying to convince people to visit serial killers in jail. Sometimes they were writers or tabloid reporters, grad students, the merely morbid, or even a couple of psychics. I wondered why they always came in pairs, and what her partner was thinking as he stood behind her, silent. Only the sleaziest ones came after me like this, not asking Paul or Janet's permission, waiting for a time when I was alone.

Mama kept sending these people to talk to me, to persuade me to come visit her. I suspected that what she really wanted was a good look at my face so she'd know whom to come after if she ever got out.

"She misses you."

I turned my face up to the sky. "Tell her I miss Aunt Genna."

"You don't really want me to tell her that, do you?"

I closed my eyes. "You're taping this, aren't you?"

"Lisa," the woman held onto my arm when I tried to sit up. "Lisa, listen—it would only take a day, just one day out of your life. She only wants to see you—"

I jerked my arm away and ran for the house just as Janet came out.

"Who are they?"

The man and the woman were already leaving. They could try all they liked. I wasn't ready to see Mama and maybe never would be. But I didn't want any questions either. "Just Jehovah's Witnesses."

I saw the woman waiting outside school the next day but pretended not to notice her. Eventually she went away.

I was fourteen when I first tried to commit suicide. I remember it clearly because it was New Year's Eve. Paul and Janet were at a costume ball and thought I was with a friend. Paul was a pirate and Janet was a princess.

They drove me to my friend's house. Paul put his eye patch on his chin so it wouldn't bother him while he drove. I sat in the back, at peace with myself. In my mind I was seeing my foster parents at my funeral, standing grief-stricken at the open casket, gazing down at my calm face.

When they let me off, I walked back home. I brought all Janet's Midol and all Paul's stomach pills upstairs to my bedroom, where I had already stashed two bottles of aspirin. I went back down to get three bottles of ginger ale and a large plastic tumbler.

Then I wrote a poem for Paul and Janet. It was three pages long. At the time it seemed epic and moving, but now I squirm when I think about it. I'm glad I didn't die. What a horrible piece of writing to be remembered by. It was something out of a soap opera: "My Darling Parents, I must leave / I know you will, but you must not grieve" sort of thing. I guess it wouldn't have been so bad if I hadn't made everything rhyme.

I emptied the aspirin into a cereal bowl. Deciding to get it all over with at once, I stuffed a handful into my mouth. God, the taste. Dusty, bitter aspirin crunched in my mouth like hard-shelled bugs. My gag reflex took over, and I lost about twenty aspirin on my quilt. I chugalugged three cups of ginger ale to get the taste out of my mouth, then went more slowly and swallowed the pills one by one.

After the twenty-sixth aspirin, I stopped counting and concentrated on not throwing up. I didn't have enough money to get more, and I didn't want to waste anything. When I got to the bottom of the cereal bowl, I'd had enough. I'd also run out of ginger ale. Bile was leaking into my mouth. Much later, I discovered that overdosing on aspirin is one of the worst ways to go. Aspirin is toxic, but the amount needed to kill a grown adult is so high that the stomach usually bursts before toxicity kicks in.

My last moments on earth. I didn't know what to do with them. Nothing seemed appropriate. I lay on my bed and read *People* magazine. Farrah was seeing Ryan O'Neal. Some model was suing Elvis's estate for palimony. Disco was dying. A Virginia woman was selling Belgian-chocolate-covered caramel apples at twelve dollars apiece to stars who said they had never tasted anything so wonderful.

At midnight I heard the fireworks but was too tired to get out of bed. I drifted into sleep, my ears ringing so loud I could barely hear the party at our neighbor's house next door.

Some time during the night, I crawled to the bathroom at the end of the hall and vomited thin strings of yellow bile into the toilet.

All the next week I wished I had died. My stomach could hold nothing down. Janet thought it was a stomach flu and got me a bottle of extra-strength Tylenol and some Pepto-Bismol. To this day, I can't stand the taste of ginger ale.

By some strange quirk of fate, Mama came for me not long after the SPCA took Picnic away. People had complained about Picnic's affectionate behavior, and when Officer Wilkenson got involved, it was the end.

Aunt Genna was weeping quietly upstairs in her bedroom when the doorbell rang. She was always telling me not to let strangers in, so when I saw the woman waiting on the steps, I just stared at her.

"Auntie's busy," I said.

The woman's face was smooth and pale. "Lisa," she said.
"Don't you remember me, baby?"

I backed away, shaking my head.

"Come here, baby, let me look at you," she said, crouching down. "You've gotten so big. You remember how I used to sing to you? 'A-hunting we will go'? Remember?"

Her brown eyes were familiar. Her dark blond hair was highlighted by streaks that shone in the sunlight.

"Aunt Genna doesn't like me talking to strangers," I said.

Her face set in a grim expression and I knew who she was. She stood. "Where is your aunt?"

"Upstairs," I said.

"Let me go talk to her. You wait right here, baby. When I come back, maybe we'll go shopping. We can get some cotton candy. It used to be your favorite, didn't it? Would you like that?"

I nodded.

"Stay right here," the woman said as she walked by me, her blue summer dress swishing. "Right here, baby."

Her high heels clicked neatly as she went upstairs. I sat in the hallway, on Picnic's high-backed chair. It still smelled of him, salty, like seaweed.

Something thunked upstairs. I heard a dragging sound. Then the shower started. After endless minutes, the door to the bathroom creaked open. Mama's high heels clicked across the floor again.

"I'm back!" Mama said cheerfully, bouncing down the stairs. "Your aunt says we can go shopping if you want. She's taking a bath." Mama leaned down and whispered, "She wants to be alone."

She had my backpack over one shoulder. I jumped down from the chair. Mama held out her hand. I hesitated.

"Coming?" she said.

"I have to be back tonight," I said. "I'm going to Jimmy's birthday party."

"Well then," she said. "Let's go buy him a present."

She led me to her car. It was bright blue and she let me sit up front. I couldn't see over the dashboard because she made me wear a seat belt. Aunt Genna's house shrank as we drove away. I remember wondering if we were going to get another dog now that Picnic was gone. I remember looking down at Mama's shoes and seeing little red flecks sprayed across the tips like a splatter paint I'd done in kindergarten. I remember Mama giving me a bad-tasting orange juice, and then I remember nothing.

"Yuck," I said. "I'm not touching it."

"No problem," Amanda said. "I'll do it."

Amanda was everyone's favorite lab partner because she'd do absolutely anything, no matter how gross. We looked down at the body of a dead fetal pig that Amanda had chosen from the vat of formaldehyde. We were supposed to find its heart.

"Oh, God," I said, as Amanda made the first cut.

For a moment, I was by the lake and Mama was smearing blood on my cheeks.

"Now you're a real woman," she said. Goose bumps crawled up my back.

"I don't know how you can do that," I said to Amanda.

"Well, you put the knife flat against the skin. Then you press. Then you cut. It's very simple. Want to try?"

I shook my head and crossed my arms over my chest.

"Chickenshit," Amanda said.

"Better than being a ghoul," I said.

"Just my luck to get stuck with a wimp," she muttered loud enough for me to hear as she poked around the pig's jellied innards, looking for a small purple lump.

I sat on my lab stool feeling stupid while Amanda hunched over the pig. Not all the chopping and dismemberment in the world could make her queasy. Mama would have liked her. She straightened up then and shoved the scalpel in my face, expecting me to take it from her.

At that moment, I saw the scars on her wrists. When she noticed me staring, she pulled her sleeve down to cover them.

"I slipped," she said defensively. "And cut myself."

We faced each other, oblivious to the murmur of the class around us.

"Don't you say anything," she said.

Instead of answering, I unbuttoned the cuff of my blouse and rolled it up my arm. I turned my hand over so the palm was up.

The second time I tried to commit suicide was when I was fifteen, a year after my attempt with the aspirin. This time I had done my homework. I knew exactly what I was going to do.

I bought a straight-edged razor.

Janet and Paul were off to the theater. I waved them goodbye cheerfully as they raced through the rain to the car.

I closed the front door and listened to the house. Then I marched upstairs and put on my bikini. I ran a bath, putting in Sea Foam bubble bath and mango bath oil. I stepped into the tub, then lay back slowly, letting the water envelop me as I watched the bathroom fill with steam.

The razor was cold in my hands, cold as a doctor's stethoscope. I held it underwater to warm it up. Flexed my arms a few times. Inhaled several deep breaths. Shut the water off. It dripped. There was no way I could die with the tap dripping, so I fiddled with that for a few minutes.

Got out of the tub. Took a painkiller. Got back in the tub. Placed the razor in the crook of my elbow. Hands shaking. Pushed it down. It sank into my skin, the tip disappearing. I felt nothing at first. I pulled the razor toward my wrist, but halfway down my forearm the cut began to burn. I yanked the razor away.

Blood welled in the cut. Little beads of blood. I hadn't gone very deep, just enough for the skin to gape open slightly. Not enough to reach a vein or an artery.

I was shaking so hard the bubbles in the tub were rippling. The wound felt like a huge paper cut. I clutched it, dropping the razor in the tub.

"I can do it," I said, groping for the razor.

I put it back in the same place and pushed deeper. A thin stream of blood slithered across my arm and dripped into the tub. It burned, it burned.

Paul and Janet came home and found me in front of the TV watching Jimmy Stewart in *It's a Wonderful Life*. It always makes me cry. So there I was, bawling as Paul and Janet came through the door. They sat on either side of the armchair and they hugged me.

"What is it, honey?" Paul kissed my forehead.

"No, really, I'm okay. It's nothing." I said.

"You sure? You don't look okay," Janet said.

I rested my head on her knees, making her dress wet. Paul and Janet said they wanted to know everything about me, but there were things that made them cringe. What would they do if I said, "I'm afraid Mama will find me and kill me"?

"I'm such a marshmallow. I even cry at B.C. telephone commercials," is what I said.

Paul leaned over and smoothed my hair away from my face. "You know we love you, don't you, Pumpkin?"

He smelled of Old Spice and I felt like I was in a commercial. Everything would be perfect, I thought, if only Canada had the death penalty.

In a tiny, grungy antique store in Masset on the Queen Charlotte Islands I found the moose. Paul and Janet had brought me with them to a business convention. Since the finer points of Q-Base accounting bored me silly, I left the hotel and wandered into the store.

Nature pictures and small portraits of sad-eyed Indian children cluttered the wall. The hunchbacked owner followed me everywhere I went, saying nothing. Not even hello. I was about to leave when I saw the moose.

"How much is that?" I asked, reaching for it.

"Don't touch," he grunted at me.

"How much?" I said.

"Twenty."

I handed him the twenty dollars, grabbed the picture, and left.

"What on earth is that?" Janet asked when I got back. She was at the mirror, clipping on earrings.

"Oh, nothing. Just a picture."

"Really? I didn't know you were interested in art. Let me see."

"It's just a tacky tourist picture. I'll show it to you later."

"Here," Janet said, taking the package from my hands and unwrapping it.

"Careful." I said.

"Yes, yes." Janet's mouth fell open and she dropped the picture onto the bed. "Oh my God, that's disgusting! Why on earth did you buy it? Take it back."

I picked up the picture and hugged it to my chest. She tried to pry it from me, but I clung to it tightly. Paul came in and Janet said, "Paul, get that disgusting thing out of here!"

She made me show it to him and he laughed. "Looks very Dali," he said.

"It's obscene."

"This from the woman who likes Pepsi in her milk."

"Paul, I'm serious," she hissed.

"Let her keep it," Paul said. "What harm can it do?"

Later I heard him whisper to her, "Jan, for God's sake, you're overreacting. Drop it, all right? All right?"

I still have it, hanging in my bathroom. Except for the moose lying on its side, giving birth to a human baby, it's a lovely picture. There are bright red cardinals in the fir trees, and the sun is beaming down on the lake in the left-hand corner. If you squint your eyes and look in the trees, you can see a woman in a blue dress holding a drawn bow.

Amanda's house was the kind I'd always wanted to live in. Lace curtains over the gabled windows, handmade rugs on the hardwood floors, soft floral chairs, and dark-red cherry furniture polished to a gleam.

"You like it?" Amanda said, throwing her coat onto the brass coat stand. "I'll trade you. You live in my house and I'll live in yours."

"I'd kill to live here," I said.

Amanda scratched her head and looked at the living room as if it were a dump. "I'd kill to get out."

I followed her up the stairs to a large, airy room done in pale pink and white. I squealed, I really did, when I saw her canopied bed. Amanda wore a pained expression.

"Isn't it revolting?"

"I love it!"

"You do?"

"It's gorgeous!"

She tossed her backpack into a corner chair. I flopped down on the bed. Amanda had tacked a large poster to the underside of her canopy—a naked man with a whip coming out of his butt like a tail.

"It's the only place Mother let me put it," she explained. "Cute, huh?"

Downstairs, a bass guitar thumped. A man shrieked some words, but I couldn't make them out. Another guitar screeched, then a heavy, pulsating drumbeat vibrated the floor. Then it stopped.

"Matthew," Amanda said.

"Matthew?"

"My brother."

Amanda's mother called us to dinner. Matthew was already heading out the door, wearing a kilt and white body makeup. His hair was dyed black and stood up like the spikes on a blowfish. When his mother wasn't looking, he snatched a tiny butter knife with a pearl handle and put it down his kilt. He saw me watching him and winked as he left.

"So where do your real parents come from?" Amanda's mother said, pouring more wine into cut crystal glasses.

There were only the four of us. We sat close together at one end of a long table. My face flushed. I was feeling tipsy.

"Africa," I said.

Amanda's mother raised an elegant eyebrow.

"They were killed in an uprising."

She still looked disbelieving.

"They were missionaries," I added. I took a deep drink. "Doctors."

"You don't say."

"Mother," Amanda said. "Leave her alone."

We were silent as the maid brought in a large white ceramic tureen. As she lifted the lid, the sweet, familiar smell of venison filled the room. I stared at my plate after she placed it in front of me.

"Use the fork on the outside, dear," Amanda's mother said helpfully.

But I was down by the lake. Mama was so proud of me. "Now you're a woman," she said. She handed me the heart after she wiped the blood onto my cheeks with her knife. I held it, not knowing what to do. It was as warm as a kitten.

"I think you'd better eat something," Amanda said.

"Maybe we should take that glass, dear."

The water in the lake was cool and dark and flat as glass. The bones sank to the bottom after we'd sucked the marrow. Mama's wet hair was flattened to her skull. She pried a tooth from the moose and gave it to me. I used to wear it around my neck.

"I'm afraid," I said. "She has a pattern, even if no one else can see it."

"Your stew is getting cold," Amanda's mother said.

The coppery taste of raw blood filled my mouth. "I will not be her," I said. "I will break the pattern."

Then I sprayed sour red wine across the crisp handwoven tablecloth that had been handed down to Amanda's mother from her mother and her mother's mother before that.

After a long, shimmering silence, Amanda's mother said, "I have a Persian carpet in the living room. Perhaps you'd like to shit on it." Then she stood, put her napkin on the table, and left.

"Lisa," Amanda said, clapping her hand on my shoulder. "You can come over for dinner anytime you want."

Mama loved to camp in the summer. She would wake me early, and we'd sit outside our tent and listen. My favorite place was in Banff. We camped by a turquoise lake. Mama made bacon and eggs and pancakes over a small fire. Everything tasted delicious. When we were in Banff, Mama was happy. She whistled all the time, even when she was going to the bathroom. Her cheeks were apple-red and dimpled up when she smiled. We hiked for hours, seeing other people only from a distance.

"Imagine there's no one else on earth," she said once as she closed her eyes and opened her arms to embrace the mountains. "Oh, just imagine it."

When we broke camp, we'd travel until Mama felt the need to stop and settle down for a while. Then we would rent an apartment, Mama would find work, and I would go to school. I hated that part of it. I was always behind. I never knew anybody, and just as I started to make friends, Mama would decide it was time to leave. There was no arguing with her. The few times I tried, she gave me this look, strange and distant.

I was eleven when we went through the Badlands of Alberta, and while I was dozing in the back, the car hit a bump and Mama's scrapbook fell out of her backpack.

I opened it. I was on the second page when Mama slammed on the brakes, reached back, and slapped me.

"Didn't I tell you never to touch that? Didn't I? Give it to me now. Now, before you're in even bigger trouble."

Mama used the scrapbook to start our fire that night, but it was too late. I had seen the clippings, I had seen the headlines, and I was beginning to remember.

That night I dreamed of Aunt Genna showering in blood. Mama held me until I stopped trembling.

"Rock of ages, cleft for me," Mama sang softly, as she cradled me back and forth. "Let me hide myself in thee."

I closed my eyes and pretended to sleep. Mama squeezed herself into the sleeping bag with me and zipped us up. I

waited for her to say something about the scrapbook. As the
night crawled by, I became afraid that she would never men-
tion it, that I would wait and wait for something to happen.
The waiting would be worse, far worse, than anything Mama
could do to me.

Amanda and Matthew had a game called Take It. The first
time I played, we were behind a black van in the school parking lot. They stood beside me as I rubbed a patch of skin on
my calf with sandpaper until I started to bleed. The trick to
this game is to be extremely high or just not give a shit.

Amanda squeezed lemon juice onto my calf. I looked
straight into her eyes. "Thank you," I said.

Matthew pulled a glue stick out of his schoolbag and
smeared it on my calf. "Thank you," I said.

Back to Amanda, who had been poking around in the bald
patch of earth by the parking lot and had come back with a
hairy spider as large as a quarter. It wriggled in her hands.
Fuck, I thought. Oh, fuck.

She tilted her hands toward my calf. The spider struggled
against falling, its long, thin legs scrabbling against her palm,
trying to grab something.

Long before it touched me, I knew I'd lost. I yanked my
leg back so that the spider tickled the inside of my leg as it
fell, missing the mess on my calf completely. I brought my
foot up and squashed it before anyone thought of picking it
up again.

When I was twelve, I took the Polaroid picture Officer
Wilkenson had given me to a police station in Vancouver.

In the picture, Aunt Genna and Officer Wilkenson are both blurs, but there is a little brown-haired girl in the foreground clutching a broom handle and squinting into the camera.

I showed the Polaroid to a man behind a desk. "That's my Aunt Genna," I said. "My mama killed her, but she's not in the picture."

He glanced at the picture, then at me. "We're very busy," he said. "Sit down." He waved me toward a chair. "Crazies," he muttered as I turned away. "All day long I got nuts walking in off the street."

After a while a policewoman took me to another room, where a grave-looking man in a navy-blue suit asked a lot of questions. He had a flat, nasal voice.

"So this is you, right? And you say this is Officer Wilkenson?"

He made a few calls. It all took a long time, but he was getting more and more excited. Then someone else came in and they made me say it all over again.

"I already told you. That's Aunt Genna. Yes," I said, "that's the officer. And that's me."

"Holy smokaroonies," said the navy-blue suit. "We've got her."

The third time I tried to commit suicide, I found out where Paul kept his small automatic at work. It was supposed to be protection against robbers, but it wasn't loaded and I had a hard time finding the ammunition. When he was busy with an order, I put the gun in my purse.

This time I was going to get it right.

I remember it was a Wednesday. The sky was clear and there was no moon. I didn't want to mess up Paul and Janet's house, so I was going to do it at Lookout Point, where I could watch the waves and listen to the ocean.

I left no note. Couldn't think of anything to say, really. Nothing I could explain. There was already a queer deadness to my body as I walked up the road trying to hitch a ride. This time was the last time.

Cars passed me. I didn't care. I was willing to be benevolent. They didn't know. How ironic, I thought, when Matthew pulled over and powered down his windows.

"Where to?"

"You going anywhere near Lookout?"

"I am now."

I opened the door and got in. He was surprisingly low-key for Matthew. He had on a purple muscle shirt and black studded shorts.

"Going to a party?"

"Yeah," I said. "Me and a few old friends."

Something British was on the radio. We drove, not saying anything until we came to the turnoff.

"You were supposed to go left," I said.

Matthew said nothing.

"We're going the wrong way," I said.

"Yeah?"

"Yeah. Lookout's that way."

"Yeah?"

"Matthew, quit fucking around."

"Ooh. Nasty language."

"Matthew, stop the car."

"Scared?"

"Shitting my pants. Pull over."

"You know," he said casually. "I could do anything to you out here and no one would ever know."

"I think you'd better stop the car before we both do something we might regret."

"Are you scared now?"

"Pull the car over, Matthew."

"Babe, call me Matt."

"You are making a big mistake," I said.

"Shitting my pants," he said.

I unbuttoned my purse. Felt around until the smooth handle of the gun slid into my palm. The deadness was gone now, and I felt electrified. Every nerve in my body sang.

Matthew opened his mouth, but I shut him up by slowly leveling the gun at his stomach.

"You could try to slap this out of my hand, but I'd probably end up blowing your nuts off. Do you know what dumdum bullets are, asshole?"

He nodded, his eyes fixed on the windshield.

"Didn't I tell you to stop the car?" I clicked off the safety. Matthew pulled over to the embankment. The radio played "Mr. Sandman." A semi rumbled past, throwing up dust that blew around us like a faint fog.

He lifted his finger and put it in the barrel of the gun.

"Bang," he said.

Mama would never have hesitated. She'd have enjoyed killing him.

I had waited too long. Matthew popped his finger out of

the barrel. I put the gun back in my purse. He closed his eyes, rested his head on the steering wheel. The horn let out a long wail.

I can't kill, I decided then. That is the difference. I can betray, but I can't kill. Mama would say that betrayal is worse.

A long time ago in Bended River, Manitoba, six people were reported missing:

Daniel Smenderson, 32,	last seen going out to the nearby 7-Eleven for cigarettes
Angela Iyttenier, 18,	hitchhiking
Geraldine Aksword, 89,	on her way to a curling match
Joseph Rykman, 45,	taking a lunch break at the construction site where he worked
Peter Brendenhaust, 56,	from the St. Paul Mission Home for the Homeless.
Calvin Colnier, 62,	also from the St. Paul Mission

After a snowstorm cut off power to three different subsections near Bended River, a police officer, investigating complaints of a foul smell, went to 978 West Junction Road. A little girl greeted him at the door in her nightgown. The house was hot. He could smell wood smoke from the fireplace in the living room. Chopped wood was piled to the ceiling. As he stomped the snow off his boots, he asked if her parents were home. She said her daddy was in the basement.

"Where's your mommy?" he asked.

"Gone," she said.

"How long have you been here on your own?"

She didn't answer.

"Do you know where your mommy went?" he asked.

"A-hunting we will go," the little girl sang. "A-hunting we will go. Heigh-ho the derry-oh, a-hunting we will go."

He took her hand, but she wouldn't go down to the basement with him.

"Mama says it's bad."

"How come?"

"Daddy's down there."

As he opened the door, the reek grew stronger. Covering his mouth with a handkerchief, he took a deep breath and flicked the light switch, but it didn't work. He went back to his car, radioed for backup, and was refused. The other officer on the Bended River police force was on lunch break. So he got his flashlight, then descended.

And found nothing. The smell seemed to be coming from everywhere. Nauseated, he called out, asking if anyone was down there.

The basement had neatly tiled floors. Everything sparkled under the flashlight's beam. Faintly, beneath the overpowering stench, he could smell something antiseptic, like the hospitals used. There was a large, thick butcher's block with a marble counter against the wall in the center room.

"It smelled something like rotten steaks," he told friends later. "But more like the smell my wife gets when she has her period."

There were only three rooms in the basement. A bathroom, a storeroom, and the center room with the marble counter. After checking them all twice, he noticed that the butcher's block was hinged. He heaved and strained but couldn't lift it. His fingers, though, felt a small button on one of the drawers. What did he have to lose? He pressed it.

The countertop popped up an inch. He tried to move it again and managed to slide it open. Beneath the butcher's block was a freezer. It was making no sound, no humming or purring. It was dead. The stench intensified and he thought he was going to faint.

He reached down and lifted the lid. For a moment, the skinned carcasses inside the freezer looked to him like deer or calves. Then he saw the arms and legs, sealed in extra-large plastic bags piled high.

Three days later, Moreen Lisa Rutford was charged with seven counts of murder. The bodies were identified only with difficulty, as they had no heads or fingers and Moreen refused to cooperate. The easiest to identify was David Jonah Rutford, Moreen's husband, who was missing only his heart.

Death should have a handmaiden: her pale, pale skin should be crossed with scars. Her hair should be light brown with blond streaks. Maybe her dress should only be splattered artistically with blood, like the well-placed smudge of dirt on a movie heroine's face after she's battled bad guys and saved the world. Maybe her dress should be turquoise.

She should walk beside a dark, flat lake.

In the morning, with rain hissing and rippling the lake's gray surface, a moose should rise slowly from the water, its eyes blind, its mouth dripping mud and whispering secrets.

She should raise a shotgun and kill it.

Mama wore her best dress to go calling. She sat me at the kitchen table and we ate pizza, Hawaiian, my favorite. She was cheerful that morning and I was happy because Daddy was gone so they hadn't argued. The house, for once, was quiet and peaceful.

She said, "I'm going to have to leave you alone for a bit, honey. Can you take care of yourself? Just for a little while?"

I nodded. "Yup."

"I made you some lunch. And some dinner, just in case I take too long. You know how to pour cereal, don't you?"

"Yup."

"Don't let anyone in," she said. "Don't go out. You just watch TV and Mama will be back before you know it. I got you some comics."

"Yay!" I said.

And I never saw her again until she came to get me at Aunt Genna's.

She kissed me all over my face and gave me a big hug before she left. Then she hefted her backpack onto one shoulder and pulled her baseball cap low over her face.

I watched her bounce down the walkway to the car, wave once, and drive away, smiling and happy and lethal.

Contact Sports

First Contact

They'd smoked some pot in the garage and it was already wearing off. He was getting melancholy. The high had been short and mild, barely even a buzz. Lousy skunkweed, he thought. Oh well, you get what you pay for.

Sometimes, coming down, he pretended he lived at Mike's house. It was stupid, he felt like a moron doing it. But sitting in the outdoor Jacuzzi with the portable TV blaring Sunday football, his stomach filled with the low-fat mango crepes that Patricia's part-time chef–slash–personal trainer had made for breakfast, he started to imagine what it would be like to change places with Mike.

"Fucking rain," Mike said to no one in particular.

"Language," Mike's aunt Patricia yelled from the balcony.

Mike flipped her the bird. Luckily she wasn't looking their way. Tom tilted his head. The world shifted. Maybe the

skunk had a kick after all. Mike looked very weird. Tom
stared at him. Mike had his hair slicked back and tied in a topknot. His forehead was big but his jawline came to a small
point, making him look like one of those talking animals in
The Wind in the Willows, Mr. Fox, whatever its name was.
Mike scowled at Tom. "Doesn't the sun ever come out here?"

Tom hadn't noticed the drizzle. "In about four months,
for about two days." Someone scored and the TV erupted
into cheering. The sound made him happy.

"This whole place sucks," Mike said. "Vancouver is the
shittiest place on earth."

"Unlike Toronto," Tom said, smiling.

"Fuck off, *Tommy*," Mike said.

So. Mike wanted to spread a little joy. That was the problem with getting stoned with him. He turned into such a miserable bastard. Fuck you, Tom thought. I'm having a good
time and you aren't going to spoil it. "Someone's having a
nic fit," Tom said. "Why don't you ask Patricia for a
Nicorette?"

Mike transferred his glare from Tom to the horizon and
maintained a sullen silence until Tom's mother phoned.
Patricia brought her cellular phone to the Jacuzzi.

"Tommy," his mom said, her voice tight and upset.
"Aren't you forgetting something?"

Tom instantly felt his day going downhill. The buzz van-
ished. "What?"

"Someone's coming today. You're supposed to be here."

Tom waited, puzzled.

"Your cousin," his mother said. "You said you'd be here
to meet him. You promised."

Shit, Tom thought, remembering. Him. "Yeah, yeah. I'm coming."

He hung up and sighed.

"Gotta go."

"Aww, what a shame," Mike said, almost yawning in his face. "Don't call us, we'll call you."

Patricia smiled at Tom as she took back her phone. "My Mr. Happy," she said, batting Mike's topknot back and forth. Mike swatted her hand away. In a syrupy voice she added, "Be nice or your friends won't play with you anymore."

"Boo hoo," Mike said.

Mike refused to get out of the Jacuzzi, even when Patricia shut off the bubbles. Tom changed into his sweats and waved good-bye to Patricia. When she wasn't looking, Mike flipped him the bird. Tom laughed, then flipped him one back.

He rode his bike home through the Mount Pleasant back alleys. Since the Shame-the-Johns picketers and the police cruisers had begun patrolling the area, there were fewer prostitutes around. He missed them. A couple of them had started to say hi to him.

The elevator in their apartment block was out of order, so he carried his bike up to the third floor. One of the Baker twins had spray painted the stairwells with anatomically correct pictures of impossibly proportioned comic-book women. Tom could never remember which twin was out on parole, Wayne or Willy.

Uncle Richard, his mom's latest attempt at giving him a father figure, was reading the paper in front of the TV. When Uncle Richard had started calling him Tommy, Tom started calling him Ricky and—when he found out that it really pissed him off—Ricky Ricardo. Uncle Richard slept over every Saturday. He was some kind of security guard, an ex-military type going soft around the middle. Tom's mom had encouraged them to go to baseball and hockey games, but by an unspoken agreement Tom and Uncle Richard avoided each other as much as they could. Still, his mom felt it was just a matter of time before they started repairing cars together or going fishing, God forbid.

As Tom came into the apartment, Uncle Richard looked up but said nothing.

Tom put his bike down and rolled it into the hallway closet. He lifted the bottom of his sweatshirt and wiped his forehead. On top of dealing with crappy grades and finding another job now that Chuckie Burgers was closing, Tom had Uncle Richard, who lost his temper if his toast was too dark. God, Tom thought, let him be one of her really short fucks.

His mom was waiting by the front window. He almost didn't recognize her. Her hair was no longer fire-engine red but brown and pulled back into an uncharacteristic bun. She was wearing a pastel yellow dress, too, like she was ready for ballet lessons or something. More than that, she gave off an intense nervous energy when she was sober that always took Tom by surprise. Even though she was completely still, Tom could tell that she was excited.

She glanced at him, then back out the window. "He's late. You think he's coming?"

You'd think Jesus Christ was coming, Tom thought. "He said he would."

She bit her lip nervously. Tom went over and hugged

her. She was so small he had to bend down. She patted his back, distracted.

"You eat?" Tom said.

She shook her head. "Later."

"You should eat."

"You're a good boy, Tommy." She pushed him back. "But you stink. Go take a shower."

"Don't worry, he'll come," he said.

In the shower, Tom tried to remember his cousin. Jeremy had once held a chocolate Easter bunny out of his reach until he screamed in frustration and Jeremy had started laughing. He'd been six? Seven?

Jeremy was supposed to be in the army or something. Tom's mom had been so proud she'd put up pictures of him in uniform. "Jeremy was the only one to follow his father into the military," she'd said.

"So why'd he get kicked out?" he'd said.

She'd looked at him with widened eyes, upset. He had some ideas, but no one would tell him what had really happened, not even Aunt Rhoda, the biggest mouth alive. Jeremy must have fucked up pretty bad if Rhoda wouldn't even gossip about it.

Jeremy's mother, Aunt Faith, was the only family Tom came close to liking. She sent Christmas cards and shortbread cookies that his mom waited for anxiously every year and gave them money when Mom couldn't make her paycheck stretch. But once, Aunt Faith had sat him down and explained that his mother was a fallen woman, that he'd been born out of wedlock. That was why he had epilepsy, she'd told him. God had cursed him. They'd both burn in hell unless they repented. He found he could stand her better now that she'd joined them in the family Hall of Shame.

Family was Mom. He didn't need anyone else. Especially some Bible-thumping bully.

The hot water ran out suddenly, and shivering, Tom had to rinse the soap from his hair fast. He swore and hopped out of the shower.

His mom was still by the window when he came back into the living room. Tom stood beside her and waited.

She gasped, then pointed excitedly. "Spitting image of his father," his mother said, clapping her hands. "Oh, isn't he handsome!"

Tom looked down to the street. Jeremy had stepped out of a silver convertible. Hands in his pockets, he stood at the curb looking bored and oozing cool. Tom's mother pushed the window open and waved.

"Jeremy! Up here! Yoo-hoo! Jer-e-my!"

"Mom," Tom said. "Please."

Jeremy smiled up at them and waved back.

"Go down and meet your cousin," his mother said, pushing him along. "You'll be good friends, I just know it."

Tom stayed put. Uncle Richard looked up from his newspaper and scowled at him. What was Richard so pissed about? Tom pulled himself up to his full height and, pretending indifference, left the apartment quickly. He trudged down the three flights of stairs to the lobby.

When Aunt Faith had called and asked if Jeremy could stay until he knew his way around, his mother had gladly agreed. She doesn't have to share a room with him, Tom thought. He wished his cousin was staying somewhere else. His room was barely big enough for him, much less for a cousin who could afford a car like that.

"You watch, he'll be like a brother to you," his mother had said yesterday morning when they moved the extra bed into his room.

"Mom, he's already got four brothers," Tom had said, rolling the foldaway bed into the corner of the room, near the heater. "Besides, he's twenty-one."

"So?"

Someone snagged his shirt. "Do you remember me, Tommy?"

He hadn't seen Jeremy waiting at the bottom of the stairs. "It's *Tom*," he said. "Only Mom calls me Tommy."

Jeremy cocked an eyebrow. "N-O spells no problem. Know a decent place I can park my car?"

Tom stood there for a moment. "We got a parkade. Want me to show you later?"

"Please." Jeremy held out his hand. "Looks like we're going to be bunking together. Pleased to meet you, roomie. You know, I used to babysit you."

You and half a million other people. Tom reached for Jeremy's suitcase but his cousin waved his hand away.

"I can handle that." Jeremy smiled down at him. "Ever driven a convertible?"

Tom's heart leapt. "No," he said, trying to keep the hope from his voice.

"You don't know what you're missing. Maybe I'll show you sometime. How about a ride?"

"Sure," he said, still trying not to sound excited. "Mom's waiting."

"We'll take her too."

They made their way upstairs. Tom's mother fluttered around Jeremy. Uncle Richard looked at him, then squinted, taking him in. Oh Lord, here it comes, Tom thought, waiting for them to break into arm wrestling or something equally moronic.

But when Richard shook Jeremy's hand he seemed satisfied. Jeremy hadn't flinched. Tom hated shaking Richard's hand. Yep, he thought, that's the way macho ex-marine assholes like Ricky Ricardo test your manhood. One good squeeze.

His mother danced when Jeremy asked her if she wanted to go for a ride. Uncle Richard grunted. They left him and went downstairs.

The three of them got into the car, Jeremy and Tom's mother in the front, with Tom squashed in the jump seat.

"You've gotten bigger," Jeremy said.

Tom wrinkled his nose. "I hope so. I was seven the last time you saw me."

"Oh, don't spoil it," his mother said.

Tom shut up.

"You guys hungry?" Jeremy asked.

"Oh yes," his mother said breathlessly.

"How about you?" Jeremy said.

Tom shrugged.

"What do you feel like, Aunt Christa?"

"Oh, anything. Please, just call me Chrissy. Everyone does."

Tom stared at her. She was beaming at Jeremy.

"How about some pizza?"

"Oh, fine. Anything, really."

"Pizza it is."

Tom hated it when she acted like this, agreeable to anything, complete doormat mode.

In the pizzeria, Tom tried to give Jeremy ten bucks.

"Your money's no good here," Jeremy said.

"I can pay my own way," Tom said.

"I know, big guy," Jeremy said. "Let me treat you. Come on, Tom. Just once. Please."

"Be good," his mother said. "Please, Tommy."

Things had already shifted so that it was Jeremy and his mom on one side and him on the other.

They sat at a table by the window. Two tables away, a couple argued, their voices hushed and sharp. Tom listened to catch what they were saying. His mother nudged him.

"Well?" Jeremy asked.

They both looked at him expectantly. He tried to figure out what they'd been talking about. His mom's eyes pleaded for him to pay attention. She'd be gone for days if he fucked up. "I guess," he said.

Jeremy leaned his elbows against the table, then rested his chin in his hands. "You guess," he said slowly. "You don't know if you're in grade ten or not?"

"He's not usually this rude," his mother said. "It's probably the medication."

Tom stared at her, surprised. She dropped her eyes and turned to the window. Jeremy watched her, then Tom.

"Relax," Tom said. "She means my anticonvulsants."

"Oh, let's talk about something else," she said, too brightly.

"You still have fits?" Jeremy said, ignoring her.

Fits? Fits? Fuck, Tom thought. He smiled pleasantly. "You still thinking about a military career?"

There was silence at the table.

"Oh, no," said Tom's mother, gushing. "Tommy doesn't have *those* anymore. Isn't that right, Tommy? I wonder where our food is? You wonder why they call it fast food when it takes forever to get here, don't you? I think it's outrageous that they can charge what they do, why in some places it's two dollars for a Pepsi! Isn't that outrageous?" His mother took a breath and stared out the window again.

When the pizza came she barely touched her slice. She kept her head down, squeezing her lips shut. Jeremy ate without stopping to talk.

On the bright side, Tom thought, this'll probably be a very short visit.

That night Tom woke and rolled over. He'd been afraid Jeremy would snore or talk in his sleep. Jeremy was awake and gazing at the ceiling. He turned to face Tom and grinned. "Always takes time to get used to a new place."

"Takes me weeks," Tom said. "Last time we moved, it took me four days to remember which way the bathroom was. I kept going into the kitchen."

Jeremy reached over to the night table for his cigarettes. "Just be glad you're not an army brat. You'd really be screwed then. We'd get used to a place, then, bam! We'd be outta there." Jeremy offered him the pack. "Want one?"

"No thanks." Tom wanted to ask his cousin why he'd

been dishonorably discharged, but it was hard to think of a polite way to bring it up. "Hey, Jeremy, I heard you killed someone" didn't seem like the right approach.

"Richard doesn't like me," Jeremy said.

"Show me one person he does like." Tom snorted. "He always acts that way."

"Not like my dad. Easygoing. Talks to everyone. Wherever we go, it's blah-blah-blah to anyone he can get hold of. An all-round nice guy."

"Richard's not my dad."

Jeremy shook a cigarette out of the pack. "Well, don't let me keep you awake. You've got school tomorrow."

"Yee-hah," Tom muttered. "I wish I could quit."

"Why don't you? Just take off. Travel the world." Jeremy spread his arms wide.

"I wish. Mom would kill me. She said she'd get someone to break my arms if I quit before I graduated."

Jeremy stared at him. "She said that to you?"

"Well, duh. She was just joking."

"What a sense of humor."

"How long are you staying?" Tom said.

"Just until I find a place. Why? Want your room back?"

"No, no. Just wondering."

"How long before school's out?"

"Months." Tom groaned theatrically.

"Got a girlfriend?"

Tom looked at Jeremy, who seemed mildly interested.

"No time," Tom said.

"But there's someone you like," Jeremy said, flicking his lighter open.

"Maybe." Tom was beginning to feel uncomfortable.

"How old is she?"

"Eighteen."

"Uh-oh. An older woman." Jeremy closed the lighter. "I remember when I was fifteen. Her name was Michelle. Michelle Latournier. God, she was gorgeous. She's married, got a kid, lives on welfare now, but back then . . ." He put his hands behind his neck and closed his eyes, an unlit cigarette dangling from the side of his mouth. "I would have died for her."

"Her name's Paulina," Tom said. "Redhead."

"Paulina Redhead. Weird name."

"No," Tom said crossly. "Her hair is red." The actual color was called strawberry-blond. Tom had heard one of the girls on the bus saying Paulina dyed her hair. Strawberry-blond. Sitting behind her at band practice, Tom had looked very carefully at her roots to see if they were really brown, but he couldn't tell. "Paulina Mazenkowski."

Jeremy started to cough. "Excuse me. Gotta quit the smokes."

Tom turned his head. It sounded suspiciously like his cousin was trying to cover laughter.

"So, have you asked her out yet?"

"Me?"

"Is there anyone else in the room?"

"No. Not in a billion years."

"I thought you said you liked her."

"Yeah, but . . ." Tom stopped.

Jeremy rolled over and leaned on one arm. "No hump," he said, looking at Tom's back. "Decent teeth. Okay complexion. Speaks English. Fairly intelligent—for a teenager. Infatuated. Willing. You've got Smurf hair, but I suppose that's cool these days. Why not?"

Tom imagined what would happen if he went up to Paulina Mazenkowski at school and asked her to go out with him. She'd laugh her head off or just sneer. Either way, he thought, closing his eyes, I'm never going to find out.

In the dream everything was dark except the ring of fire around the sun. Only he could see it. He kept trying to tell people that there was an eclipse but they looked at him as if he were insane and he realized they couldn't understand a word he was saying. What *was* he saying?

As he was waking, he remembered the real eclipse. It had happened on his birthday. He'd been very, very young. When the sky was an eerie dark blue with a wispy ring of pearl-white light at its center, the birds had stopped singing, the bees had stopped droning, and the cows in the field had lined up and headed back to the barn. Everyone else was making spooky noises. He'd put his hand in Jeremy's because Jeremy wasn't afraid. He'd felt safe.

Jeremy really was snoring now, but it was muffled because his head was under his pillow. Tom, to his surprise, didn't mind the sound. He pulled his blankets over his head and went to sleep.

Late in the morning, the aura started. He took a shower with the plastic curtain open and got the floor soaked. He knew it would drip into the apartment downstairs and Mrs. Tupper would complain to the manager, but he couldn't close the curtain, couldn't take the chance that someone would be there waiting for him. He tried extra medication, but it didn't help. Something large and dark followed him all day. He kept turning around, fast, to catch it, but there was nothing. He knew it was just the aura, but his heart still trip-hammered at loud noises. His palms sweated as he waited for someone to put a knife through his back or drop a wire around his neck and strangle him.

Later, at Chuckie Burgers, he watched the customers carefully as he did the till, half convinced that one of them was going to pull out a gun and shoot him. When a few customers looked at him strangely, he realized he was sweating hard, even though it was cold. After the dinner rush there was nothing to do. Tom mopped the men's washroom and the aura began to fade like a headache. During his last break he snuck out to the alley and smoked a joint. Sometimes it helped, sometimes it made things worse. Tonight it mellowed him out, blurred and flattened the day until it didn't bug him anymore. He squirted some Visine in his eyes and popped a few breath mints before he went back to finish his shift.

After closing, Angie, the manager, brought in a big cake shaped like a hamburger. Everyone tried to smile, but it reminded Tom of a funeral.

"Here's to Chuckie Burgers," she said.

"To Chuckie's," Tom said.

The other people muttered, drank their orange juice, grabbed their cake, and left. Tom took the letter of reference Angie gave him and carefully tucked it in his knapsack.

"You're a good worker," Angie said. "You'll find another job in no time."

Biking home, he wondered what they were going to do for next month's rent. They could sell some stuff. The tape deck wasn't half bad. The TV, well, it just wouldn't go for much. He'd already pawned the VCR.

The elevator was fixed but some joker had peed in one corner. Tom held his breath for as long as he could.

"I'm home," he said.

"Hey, Tom!"

Tom jumped, surprised at the voice until he remembered. Jeremy wandered into the living room. He looked like he'd just stepped out of *GQ*.

"It's eleven-thirty." Jeremy sounded concerned. "You been in school all this time?"

"I was at work."

"You have a job?"

"Had a job."

"Fired?" Jeremy leaned against the wall.

"Laid off. Business was slow." Tom flopped on the couch, hoping Jeremy would just go back to bed. "We got anything to eat?"

"Check the fridge."

Tom stayed on the couch, feeling his eyelids getting heavy. "In a bit."

"You okay?"

"Yeah. Where's Mom?"

"You tell me."

Shit. On vacation already. He'd thought she'd last longer.

"She must have a night shift," he lied, wishing she really was starching tablecloths at the laundry plant.

Jeremy was staring at him, so he forced himself off the couch. He opened the fridge, then stood back. "Whoa."

"I did a little shopping," his cousin said, following him into the kitchen. "You guys were running low. Least I could do."

He'd never seen the fridge like this before. It was actually crowded. The food was squashed in. "So this is ours?"

"Well, duh," Jeremy said.

Tom, annoyed, said, "I mean, you're sharing?"

"No, I'm going to eat it all myself."

"Oh," Tom said, closing the fridge.

After a pause, Jeremy said, "Sarcasm—ever heard of it?"

Embarrassed, Tom tried to think of something clever to say back. He usually wasn't so slow. "I'll eat later."

Jeremy threw his hands up. "Whatever."

As his cousin left the kitchen, Tom decided that Jeremy had been trying to be nice. He sat down at the table. The kitchen was quiet except for the hum of the refrigerator. He got up and crossed to the window. He had an urge to go for a ride but instead went to find his English assignment.

"No, no, no," Mike said, kicking some garbage into the corner before sitting on the hallway floor. "Tattooing is out. Piercing is in, man."

"Uh-huh," Tom said, kneeling down beside him.

"No, look, man," Mike said. "We got the hair, we got the clothes, we got the fucking attitude—why not go all the way?"

"What's this 'we' thing?" Tom said. He pulled out his sandwich.

"Come on. If I do it, you have to do it."

"Screw you," Tom said.

Mike stopped unwrapping his Twinkie. "I'm serious, man. What kind of experience is it going to be if we don't do it together?"

"Extremely painful. The key word being *pain*. Call me boring, call me dull, but sticking myself full of holes is not my idea of cool."

"Cool, schmool. This is about adrenaline, man. Fucking Nazis." Mike handed him a yogurt-covered low-fat granola bar. "Man, they are trying to starve me. I don't know how you can eat this shit."

Tom had wondered why Patricia kept packing granola bars when Mike never ate them. When he'd told her that Mike hated health food, she'd said he'd specifically requested it. After he thought about it for a while, he realized that Mike was giving him food in a way that wouldn't embarrass him.

"It's good for you," Tom said.

Mike made gagging sounds. "It's shit. One hundred percent organic, hand-picked, underprocessed shit."

"Unlike your Twinkie."

"Fuck off, this is manna."

Mike pushed his hair back but the bangs flopped down again, covering half his face. He handed Tom a tofu dog and an underripe papaya. They ate in silence.

His mom had come back from vacation that morning. He'd snapped awake when he'd heard the key in the lock. He'd heard her giggle, then the sound of a man's voice. A man who wasn't Uncle Richard. Yes! Tom thought as the front door closed. Her pumps clicked down the hallway to the bathroom. Usually she didn't let men into the apartment until she'd known them for a few weeks. She'd been careful ever since one of them had taken her purse, her jewelry, and the good TV while she slept. "Screwed," she'd said. "Literally and figuratively." She'd looked tough for a few seconds before she'd burst out crying and put her head in her hands.

"Think about it," Mike said.

It took Tom a few moments to realize that he was back on body piercing. "Like anyone's going to hire me with a pierced nose."

"Fuck," Mike said. "Look at you, man. Your hair's enough to scare off respectable people."

"I tie it back," Tom said.

Mike rolled his eyes. "Hel-lo! Which one of us has blue-berry fucking Kool-Aid hair? What's a fucking nose ring to that?"

"You first."

"Wuss," Mike said.

The buzzer rang. Mike kicked the last of his lunch into the corner. "What you got?"

"Physics," Tom said, yawning.

"Later," Mike said. He punched Tom in the arm and left.

After a week Tom was used to finding Jeremy lounging around the living room when he got home from school.

"Don't you go anywhere but your room?" Jeremy asked as Tom came through the door.

Tom put his bike away.

Jeremy popped his head around the corner. "Don't you have any friends?"

"What?"

"Friends," Jeremy said this very slowly, like he was talking to an idiot. "Guys you bum around with. You know, guys you go to the pool hall with, smoke with, check out girls with. I can look it up in the dictionary if you like."

"Bug off," Tom said.

"Just ragging you, kid," Jeremy said as he went back into the living room and sprawled out on the lounger, remote control in one hand, a can of Pepsi in the other. "How'd school go?"

"Okay. Did Mom leave me any money?"

Jeremy shook his head.

"Are you sure?" Tom flopped down on the sofa. "She said she might."

"She didn't. How much do you need?"

"Seventy-five bucks," Tom said glumly.

"That all? I can cover that."

"You would?" Tom hadn't considered asking Jeremy.

"Sure. What's it for?"

"Band trip. We're going to stay over two nights and we have to pay for food and stuff."

Jeremy reached into his jeans and pulled out his wallet. "I seem to remember you saying you had no time." He waved the money in front of him. "Any reason for this sudden change?"

"No," Tom said, blushing furiously.

"Paulina wouldn't happen to be in band, would she?"

"That's none of your business."

Jeremy slowly, making a great show of it, put the money back in his wallet. He turned the TV up and ignored Tom.

"Maybe she is," Tom said.

"What does she play?" Jeremy said, still not looking at him. Tom fumed. "Flute."

"Second flute? Third?"

"First."

"Is she any good?"

"Yes."

"How close do you sit to her?"

"Behind her." Tom watched desperately as Jeremy flipped through the channels. "I'd pay you back."

"Don't worry," Jeremy said. "It's no skin off my nose."

"No, really. As soon as I get another job."

"Yeah, right," Jeremy said. "Here. Take it."

Tom ignored the money. "What's that supposed to mean?"

"Let's just say I'm not going to hold my breath until I get it back."

Tom grabbed his knapsack and stood, saying nothing as he left the room.

"Not now," his mother said when she came home. She rubbed her feet and pulled off the smock of her uniform. "Next year, Tom. We'll have money next year."

When he was dressing to go out, Jeremy winked at Tom. "Think about it. It's just a lousy seventy-five bucks," he said, putting on his carefully ironed silk shirt. The shirt alone, Tom thought, could pay their electric bill.

"I don't need your charity," Tom said.

"Yeah?" Jeremy said. "Could have fooled me."

Tom turned over and faced the wall until Jeremy left. When he heard the front door slam, Tom rolled onto his back and stared at the ceiling. He lay in bed, thinking and waiting.

Jeremy came home late. Tom listened closely as he rummaged through the kitchen, opening and closing doors and rattling cutlery.

"I can wash your car!" Tom burst out as Jeremy came through the bedroom door.

"Christ!" Jeremy said, almost dropping his sandwich. "You want to give me a fucking heart attack?"

"I'm sorry. I'm really, really sorry."

"Yeah, yeah. So," he said, turning on the light. "You want to wash my car."

That Saturday Jeremy woke Tom up at seven. They drove to the nearest gas station. It was too cold for it, but Tom asked Jeremy to put the top down. He wished Mike could see him. When they got to the gas station, Jeremy pulled out the cleaning equipment. Tom groaned.

"We don't need all that, do we?" he said.

Jeremy said, "You want the money?"

First, the car was rinsed (in the shade, never in the sun), then washed (warm soapy water and a natural sea sponge). Then it was rinsed again (careful that no gravel or sand had gotten on the sponge) before it was rubbed dry (soft cotton cloth). After that, the car was waxed. Tires scrubbed. Seats and floors vacuumed. Windows washed (inside, then outside, never the other way around). Dashboard dusted (never washed). Trying to lighten Jeremy's grim concentration, Tom splashed him with the hose. But the second the water hit Jeremy's T-shirt Tom knew he'd made a mistake.

Jeremy looked up slowly.

"Oops," Tom said, putting the hose down. "Sorry."

Jeremy advanced. Tom backed away, putting the car between them.

"Come here," Jeremy said, beckoning with his finger. "Come here, Tom."

"I said I was sorry!"

"I'm not going to hurt you. I just want to talk to you. Come here, come on."

After the fourth time around the car, Jeremy charged, and Tom tripped on the hose. Jeremy yanked him up and held him by the collar.

"You're going to wash my car once a week," he said, pulling Tom close. "Every week. Until I leave."

"Jump off a bridge," Tom said. "I don't want your money anymore."

"You will do it," Jeremy said.

"Or what?"

"Or I will go to your school. I will find Paulina." He leaned toward Tom's ear and whispered, "And I will tell her everything you've told me."

Tom stood completely still, furious.

"And a few things you didn't," Jeremy added, laughing.

"Well, Tom," his cousin said before he went out that night. "Looks like you have a job."

It wasn't too bad, really. Jeremy bought groceries, cleaned up after himself, and minded his own business most of the time. He'd disappear once in a while and return when he was strung out. It must be genetic, Tom thought.

His mom really did have the night shift tonight. She kissed Jeremy on the cheek to thank him for buying dinner, even though she'd been too hungover to eat much. After she left, Tom finished his homework in the kitchen, then did the dishes.

"Where you going?" Jeremy said from the living room as Tom wheeled his bike from the closet.

"Out," Tom said, kicking the bike stand up.

"Where?"

Tom heard the lounger squeal as Jeremy got out of it. He bit back a "None of your damn business" and made himself calm by closing his eyes. "Just for a ride."

"This late?"

"It's only twelve-thirty."

"It's late," Jeremy said. He was standing in front of the door with his arms crossed. "And it's a school night."

The trick, he remembered Mike saying, is to believe you're unstoppable. "I'm going for a ride. Get out of my way."

"Go to bed. Do not pass Go, do not collect two hundred dollars."

Tom pushed the bike forward, right to Jeremy's feet, then stopped. Jeremy looked down at him.

Tom said, "You got no right to tell me what to do. You're not my father. You're not even my brother. You're some guy who's too cheap to get his own place."

Jeremy's face froze. "I'm trying to help."

"We don't need your help."

"You moron," Jeremy said. "Do you know what kind of freaks are out there?"

Tom reached for the door and Jeremy slid out of the way. "I can take care of myself."

He expected Jeremy to stop him, but he didn't.

Tom didn't bike far, just to the little park off Fraser that the city had created out of a traffic intersection. Tom sat on the swings.

It started to rain, a blotchy, half-hearted drizzle. He liked the color of wet concrete at night, the smell of the grass and dust, and the way the traffic hissed by.

A prostitute he hadn't seen before was smoking on a nearby bench. She eyed him suspiciously for a moment, then ignored him. Only one or two of the women had ever talked to him. He didn't mind. It felt better to be sitting with someone than to be sitting alone.

When she left, the park felt empty and he wanted to go home. Instead he stayed. No one, not even his mom, told him what to do. If he wanted to go riding at midnight, that was his business. He wasn't a kid anymore. He knew what he was doing. Besides, this was Vancouver, for Christ's sake, not New York.

He stayed in the park another half hour, figuring that Jeremy would be asleep.

When he got home, Jeremy was sitting at the kitchen table with a calculator. He didn't look up, though Tom went and stood beside him. He had papers scattered around him. Tom looked closer and saw that they were bills—the electric bill, phone, rent. The shoe box he kept them in was lying on the floor.

"What are you doing?"

Jeremy punched the calculator buttons. "You can take care of yourself, can you?"

"Those are private!" Tom said.

"How much are you in the hole?"

"None of your goddamn business! Get out!"

"Sit down," Jeremy said calmly.

"Get the fuck out! Get! Out!"

Jeremy finally looked up at him. "They're cutting your power off in three days. What are you going to do?"

"I can't believe you went through my things," Tom said.

"Your things? Have you told your mother?"

"Jeez," said Tom, grabbing the bills, shoving them back into the shoe box. "Don't. She can't . . . she just, she's going through a rough time. Just leave her alone."

Jeremy tweaked the shoe box and pulled. Tom pulled back, then let go, and Jeremy slid the box over to his side of the table. "Sit," he said. "Sit."

Tom reached for one of the chairs. He sat down, closing his eyes for a moment. When he opened them, Jeremy was staring at him. "I don't want you to tell Mom. It's okay. I'm handling it."

"How?" Jeremy held up Tom's medical bills. Tom flinched. Jeremy opened his wallet. Then he covered the bills in fifties. Jeremy spread out the last electric bill, the phone bill, the notice of back rent due, his mom's Mastercard and did the same thing. When Jeremy had finished, he looked at Tom. "Do I have your attention?"

Tom swallowed, unable to take his eyes off the money. How much money was on the table? Two, three thousand dollars? God, where did he get that kind of cash?

"Earth to Tommy. Do I have your attention?"

"Yes," Tom said quietly.

"Then let's make a deal," Jeremy said, suddenly cheerful.

Tom felt alarm creep along his spine. It had to be a fucking sick joke.

"What kind of deal?"

Jeremy smiled. "Remember what you said before you left? How you don't need my help?"

Tom said nothing but he knew his face was flushed.

"Oh, I don't hold grudges." Jeremy winked. "Don't get mad, get even, that's my motto. Look, it's really very simple. I'll pay off your bills, one bill a week, and I'll help with rent and food, and all you have to do is one itty bitty little thing."

Tom said cautiously, "What?"

"Oh, it's simple. All I want you to do is be good."

Tom stared at him suspiciously. "When you say 'good,' what do you mean?"

"No more sneaky wandering around at night alone. No staying overnight anywhere without phoning. You ask me if you can stay somewhere. You ask me if you can go to parties. You listen to me when I tell you what to do."

Tom had to suppress his annoyance. "But—"

"No buts." Jeremy leaned forward. "Do we have a deal?"

It was tempting. A little freedom lost. A little financial security gained. Just long enough to finish classes without worrying about rent. If his cousin wanted to play Mother Teresa, who was he to say no?

"I guess."

Jeremy got up and clapped him on the back. "Good choice. You won't regret it. Now get to bed. See? Is that so bad?"

Tom pushed back his chair and stood, feeling light-headed. He went to the bathroom, locked the door to make sure he had a few minutes to be alone, to think. He brushed his teeth absently, staring at himself in the mirror. How bad could it be?

That Saturday, Tom lay in bed reading. His arms hurt. Shoulders ached. Five hours of washing Jeremy's stupid car, scrubbing the goddamn apartment floors, and being Jeremy's fucking maid. Jeremy could take his money and shove it. There was no way he was going to spend another day like this.

Jeremy knocked. Tom knew it was Jeremy because his mom never knocked before entering a room. Frowning, he hunched down and stared at the book, no longer seeing the words.

"Still sore at me?" Jeremy said cheerfully.

Tom flipped the page.

" 'Yes, Jeremy'," Jeremy said in a high, squeaky voice. " 'I still hate your guts.' " Jeremy sat on the bed. In his normal voice he continued, "What if I asked you if you wanted to go for a ride?" He stood up. " 'Well, I don't know. I'd have to ask my mom.' "

"Go away," Tom said, turning so Jeremy wouldn't see his face.

"It speaks!"

Tom clenched his mouth shut.

" 'I've finished all my homework and I don't have a thing to do, Jeremy.' " Jeremy punched Tom's leg. "Well, let's go then."

Tom put his fingers in his ears.

"It's been a whole hour since you talked to me," Jeremy said sadly. "If you don't say something soon, I'm going to just die."

"Get lost," Tom said.

"Well. Happy birthday, kid." Then, casually, "I got you a present. Curious?"

"No." Tom flipped a page.

"It's bigger than a bread box."

Tom slammed the book shut. He glared at Jeremy and moved to get off the bed. Jeremy, laughing, grabbed his arms and pushed him down.

"Let go!" Tom said, struggling.

"Hah! It speaks again!" Jeremy straddled Tom's chest, pinning him to the bed. "And if it knows what's good for it, it will keep speaking!"

"Get off me!"

Jeremy hummed and pretended to clean his nails.

Tom bucked, kicked, even tried to bite. Jeremy yawned. "Ready to talk?"

"If you don't get off me now—"

"You'll do what?" Jeremy said, not moving. "Run and tell Mommy?" Jeremy reached over and picked up the book. *"Temporal Lobe Epilepsy, Mania, Schizophrenia, and the Limbic System.* Some light reading, huh? Jesus, don't you ever read anything normal? Ever heard of Stephen King?"

Tom stopped struggling. "What do you want?"

Jeremy smiled. "That's more like it. Let's see. Well, first, do you want to go for a ride?"

"No."

"*Meep.* Wrong answer," Jeremy reached down and pulled Tom's shirt up.

"What're you doing?"

"Let's try that again. Do you want to go for a ride?"

"No!"

"*Meep.* Wrong again. Last chance." Jeremy poked Tom hard in the side. Tom wriggled. Jeremy rubbed his hands together, chuckling. "Oh goody. Ticklish. Perfect. Now, are we going for a ride?"

Tom wrenched an arm free. He hit Jeremy, who grunted and fell back. Tom rolled, twisting loose only to be caught and pushed back onto the bed again, this time on his stomach. Jeremy leaned close and whispered, "*Meep.* Wrong again. You lose, bozo."

No one had ever tickled Tom before. Jeremy was ruthless. When Jeremy finished with him, his ribs felt bruised and he was panting heavily, almost crying.

"Let's try that one more time," Jeremy said brightly. "Does Tommy want to go for a ride?"

Tom rested, trying to catch his breath.

Jeremy lightly touched Tom's side.

"Yes!" he said quickly. "Yes!"

"That's more like it! Now, does Tommy forgive Jeremy for everything? Hmmm?"

"Yes."

"Tommy's not going to sulk anymore, is he?"

"No."

"Is Tommy sure?" Jeremy squeezed Tom's ribs.

"Yes. Don't, Jeremy. Please."

"Pretty please?"

Tom gritted his teeth. "Pretty please."

"I get the feeling that you aren't being sincere," Jeremy

said gravely. "If you are really, sincerely sorry for being such a pain in the butt, I think you'll want to prove it, won't you, Tommy?"

Tom closed his eyes and took a deep breath. Then another. And another. Jeremy bounced on him. "You awake?"

"Goddamn—"

Jeremy started tickling him again, shouting, "Say Super-califragilisticexpialidocious! Say it! Say it or I won't stop!"

Desperate, Tom shouted, "Mom!" but it didn't come out very loud. He couldn't catch his breath. Jeremy stopped for a moment.

Tom said, "Super. Cali. Expe. Fragi . . ." Fuck, he thought, what comes next? "Lista. Dextro—"

"All of it," Jeremy said, touching Tom's sides. "The word, whole word, and nothing but the word. No cheating!"

"I can't remember it! Please, Jere—"

Jeremy hooted and let Tom up. He was laughing as Tom tucked his shirt back into his pants. Tom stood and made toward the door.

"*Meep*," Jeremy said. "Wrong move. Get back here."

Tom froze, fists clenched by his sides.

"Get back here, Tommy."

"What do you want?" he said, not turning around.

"Come on. That's it. Be good. Sit."

Tom sat stiffly on Jeremy's bed. Jeremy sat beside him and put an arm around his shoulder. Tom shrugged it off.

"*Meep*," Jeremy said. He put his arm over Tom's shoulder again and this time Tom did nothing. "Come on, relax.

As long as you're good, you've got nothing to worry about. Now. Are we going to be good?"

Tom nodded miserably.

"Get your dancing shoes on, then, we're going riding!" Jeremy jumped up, pulling Tom with him. "I'm taking birthday boy out for a ride," he said as they strolled past the living room.

"Have a good time," his mother said. "Don't stay out too late."

Tom opened his mouth to yell for help, but Jeremy pushed him ahead. In the parking lot, Tom broke away from him and ran. Jeremy caught him and hissed, "*Meep.*"

"You can't do this," Tom said, as Jeremy twisted one arm up behind his back. "This is kidnapping."

"*Meep*-badda-*meep-meep*," Jeremy sang. "*Meep-meep.*"

"Goddamn you."

Jeremy laughed. He swept the car door open for Tom. "Sit," he said. Tom sat. Jeremy slammed the door shut and got in on the other side. "No tricky getting out of moving cars, no sneaky jumping out at red lights, and put your seat belt on."

Singing, Jeremy made his usual noisy exit from the parking lot.

"Can't you drive like a normal person?" Tom said.

"Tommy's sul-king," Jeremy said in a warning tone.

They drove in silence. Jeremy popped a cassette in the tape deck, and Bob Seger and the Silver Bullet Band started playing midsong.

"Aren't you curious about your present?"

Tom was silent.

" 'Of course I'm curious, Jeremy! What'd you get me, what'd you get me?' " Jeremy said in his squeaky voice. "Well, kid. It's pretty darn terrific, if I do say so myself. 'What is it? What is it?' I can't tell you. It's a surprise. 'Give me hint, give me a hint.' Well, it's bigger than a bread box. It's very soft. And Mike McConnell has one. 'Wouldn't happen to be leather would it?' Why, Tommy! How'd you guess?"

Tom's eyes widened. "You're lying."

"Unless, of course, you don't want it?"

"You're just fucking with my head."

Jeremy laughed. He looked over and saw Tom's face and went serious for a moment. Reaching across the seat, he poked him. "Let's try that again. Would I tease the birthday boy?"

"Ye—" Tom clamped his mouth shut as Jeremy held up his index finger and waggled it at him.

"You're quick. Let no one tell you that you are slow. If I remember, you said he bought it at the Leather Ranch. I am correct, aren't I?"

"Yes," he said, half-believing that Jeremy was serious.

"And that mall over there contains one store appropriately called the Leather Ranch, does it not?"

"Yes. Jeremy?" Tom said, hesitating, not knowing how to ask the question without sounding rude. Why would you buy me a leather jacket?

"Yeah?"

"I've got homework. I have to—"

"Oh, forget that tonight. We're going to have a good time."

They parked and Jeremy walked him to the mall, holding him just above the elbow. "Wouldn't want you to get lost. Now. Rules of the game. One. You pick a jacket. Two. I approve of the jacket. Three. You don't look at the price tags on any of them. Do you understand these rules?"

"But, Jerem—"

Jeremy pressed hard on a nerve in Tom's arm. "Do you understand these rules?"

When Jeremy stopped pressing, Tom said, "Yes."

"Good. Rule four. I buy. You shop. I will give you the signal—*meep*—if you are seen to be breaking a rule. If you are foolish enough to ignore the signal, I will throw you on the ground and tickle you until you pee. Is that clear?" He squeezed again.

"Yes." Tom had thought Jeremy would let go of him when they got in the mall, but Jeremy didn't.

"If you get more than four signals, I will throw you down on the floor and tickle you until you pee. Any questions?"

Tom shook his head.

"Good. You know, I like being older," Jeremy said cheerfully. "It's a far, far better thing. You're lucky you don't have any older brothers. Mine drove me nuts."

Once in the store, Jeremy sat down by the cashier, a pretty blond who covered her mouth when she giggled. He waved his hand at Tom and told him to shop. Tom immediately found a black leather bomber exactly like Mike's. He brought it to Jeremy, who told him to try it on.

"Ack," Jeremy said. "N-O spells no. Take it away."

"But I like—"

"*Meep.*"

The cashier giggled, looking at Jeremy from under her lashes. Tom wandered through the store, picking up, then putting jackets down. Jeremy finally came searching for him, saying time was a-wasting. Out of habit, Tom picked up a price tag, and Jeremy yelled triumphantly, "*Meep!* Two more, kid, and you're dead in the water."

Hardly even looking, Tom grabbed a jacket and showed it to Jeremy.

"Not bad." He turned in the direction of the cashier. "Do you have it in brown?" he called to her.

"I want black."

"It's not your color. Look in the mirror. Makes you look sick."

For the first time since entering the store, Tom glanced at a mirror. He turned away quickly.

"It's not that bad," Jeremy said. "You're not Frankenstein, you know."

Tom stared at his sneakers.

"You just wear geeky clothes and have geeky hair."

"That's all, huh?"

"Come on, stop being so hard on yourself."

"Here we go," the cashier chirped. "I got it in a size bigger because you're going to grow soon." She tilted her head as she smiled at him. "My brother was the same way exactly. He didn't grow until he was almost seventeen. You shouldn't be losing sleep about it, hey."

Tom shoved Jeremy. "Why don't you tell her about Paulina while you're at it."

Jeremy rocked on his heels and looked guiltily at the ceiling. The cashier giggled.

"You didn't."

"Who's it going to hurt? You aren't going to tell anyone, are you, Sherrie?"

"Lips are sealed."

"See? Come on, try it on." Jeremy held the jacket open. When Tom did nothing, Jeremy smiled wickedly. "In two seconds, you are going to be one meep away from total humiliation."

"You," Tom said, putting his arms in the sleeves. "Are such a crazy jerk it's not fucking funny."

"Yeah, yeah. Ta-da! You look great! All you need now is a decent haircut. Know a hairdresser open, Sherrie?"

"Sure. Try Shear Energy. Two stores down. Ask for Linda. She's the absolute."

"Wait a minute," Tom said, stopping. "I don't want a haircut."

"Don't worry about it. The jacket's free and you can pay me back for the haircut later." Jeremy paid for the jacket. Sherrie gave him her phone number. Jeremy dragged Tom into Shear Energy.

"I like my hair—Jeremy are you listening?" Tom said.

"Don't whine. God, it's grating. Hi! One haircut for my brother here, with Linda. Is she in?"

Linda had a neat platinum blond bob. She was wearing a pink suit so ugly it had to be expensive. Her fingernails were the same color as her pumps and her hair. Tom mouthed "No" at Jeremy, who whispered, "One meep and counting."

Tom listened in horror as Linda and Jeremy decided how he should look. For three terrifying seconds, Jeremy wanted a perm and a dye job, but Linda shook her head.

"Not enough time." She lifted Tom's chin. "I think we shave the back, yes, but leave the bangs. Yes, that's good."

Jeremy shook his head. "Negative. You'd still see the crappy blue stuff he's got in his hair. I want it all out."

"No way!" Tom yelled.

"How about this?" she said, pointing to a picture.

Jeremy considered it. "Yes. Yes, I like that."

"What? Let me see," Tom said.

"Here. Blunt cut. Short underneath."

"You don't need to show him. That's perfect."

"His hair."

"My money."

Linda crossed her arms over her chest. "He's unwilling, I'm unwilling."

Tom smiled in relief. The smile faded as Jeremy leaned over him. "If Tommy isn't willing, he's going to be very, very sorry. Tommy's willing, isn't he?"

"No, I'm not!"

"Oh, Tommy. You asked for this." Jeremy yanked him out of the hairdresser's chair.

"No!"

"Say yes, Tommy."

Jeremy caught him by the elbow and pressed a nerve. Tom's arm felt like a needle was going through it. "No. No. God"— Jeremy pressed hard —"damn you, no!"

"Say yes before it's too late." Slowly, Jeremy pushed him down. Then Jeremy started to tickle him.

"Help!" he shouted. Linda watched for a while, then looked away in distaste. There was no one else in the place.

Half an hour later, Jeremy clapped as Linda brushed stray hairs off Tom's neck.

"You look great, kid. Now. A white shirt. You definitely need a white shirt with that cut. What do you think, Linda?"

She nodded and fingered Tom's plaid shirt. "Burn his clothes, all of them, if they look like this."

Tom stared at his reflection. God. The person who looked back at him belonged to a debating club, got his assignments done on time, and never, ever worried about money.

"Come on, it's only hair." Jeremy cuffed him. "It'll grow back. Can I have your card, Linda? He'll be back in a month."

Jeremy bought him two white shirts, a cowboy tie, a pair of jeans (stiff dark blue Lees), a pair of pointed black leather Fluevog shoes, and eight pairs of nylon socks. Tom followed Jeremy through the stores in a daze, adding up the cost of everything Jeremy was buying him. "God," he said. "Jeremy, I can't afford this. I can't pay you back."

"Hmmm? Need any shorts?"

"No. Are you listening to me? I don't have any money. Jeremy, for fuck's sake, I—"

"Look, there's a sale. Don't worry about it, you don't have to pay me back all at once. A little here, a little there. I don't mind."

"Jeremy—"

"*Meep.* Only two meeps this time, kid. That was the first."

A headache had settled in Tom's skull. Jeremy pulled him into a jewelry store and tried to get Tom a watch but the store was closing. "Damn," Jeremy said. "We'll have to do it later." They sat on a bench in the mall and Jeremy pulled out all the receipts. Quickly he added them together and showed Tom how much he was in the hole. Jeremy grinned broadly. "Do you know what I need?"

"Yes," Tom said, appalled by the numbers on the receipts. "But I left the Ritalin at home."

"Hardy-har-har," Jeremy said. "Nope, I need some nutritional input. I know the perfect place."

They drove out to a small Japanese restaurant. Jeremy ordered for both of them. When the food arrived, Tom was relieved to see that he could recognize his meal.

"Try some sushi," Jeremy said, offering him a round roll from his plate.

Tom shook his head quickly.

"You don't know what you're missing, kid."

Jeremy joked with the waitress. Tom watched them, wishing Jeremy would shut up and let him go home. Jeremy had other ideas.

"How about a movie? Or dancing? Maybe a party?"

Tom leaned forward and put his head in his hands. "Can't we just go home?"

"I thought you liked staying up late. Give me liberty or give me death. The night is young!"

"All right, a movie," Tom said, thinking it required the least amount of energy.

"Come on then, birthday boy. Time's a-wasting! Check!"

At eleven-thirty on his sixteenth birthday, in the middle of the movie, Tom closed his eyes and fell asleep.

Second Contact

When he woke up that Sunday, Tom locked himself in the bathroom and sat on the toilet. Man, Mike was going to laugh his head off. He'd say something like, "When'd the lobotomy look come back in style, shit-for-brains?"

He could wear a baseball cap. Pull it low. But then he'd have to take it off in gym. It could blow off. Mike wouldn't be fooled, that was for sure. He got up and faced the mirror.

"Jeez," he said, running his hand through what was left of his hair.

"Tommy?" His mom knocked on the bathroom door. "Tommy, are you finished?"

"In a minute," Tom said. He wrapped his head in a towel. Fuck, this is stupid, he thought. He took the towel off and opened the door.

His mom put her hand to her mouth, a silent-screen movie star's gesture.

"That bad?"

"No," she said, starting to smile. "Oh, Tommy, it looks just fine." She reached up and touched his forehead. "I haven't seen your eyes for so long, I forgot what color they are."

Tom looked down. "I dunno. I think it's weird."

"No, it isn't. You look like a kid again."

"It's just hair."

"No, you look really good, Tommy." She pulled him forward, out of the doorway. "I've got to pee."

Tom stood in the hallway, nerving himself to face Jeremy. But when he went into the kitchen his cousin wasn't there. Tom looked in the living room and back in the bedroom, but Jeremy wasn't home.

In the kitchen Tom fixed himself some Captain Crunch. The sun was coming through the kitchen window. His mom came in and made herself toast. She was humming and kept stealing looks at him, shaking her head. She sat opposite him, reached over the table, and ruffled his hair. "I told you so."

"What?" Tom said.

"You and Jeremy. You're friends."

Tom wrinkled his nose. "I guess you could call it that."

She tried to pinch his cheek and he ducked away. "You look like your grandfather when you do that."

"Do what?"

She wrinkled her nose at him and squinted, looking peeved. "Oh, admit it. You and Jeremy are friends!"

"Mom," Tom said. But she seemed happy, and she hadn't for a long time, so he kept his mouth shut.

"—fly home soon, maybe even for Christmas, what do you think?" She smiled at him expectantly. He made himself smile, scrambling to piece together what she'd just said. "Great."

"Oh, Tommy, it'll be so much fun! You'll see. We'll get a huge tree and I'll help Mother with the turkey."

As she talked, he shrank from the thought of a family Christmas, with everyone mouthing love and good wishes and not meaning a word of it. Well, he thought, already resigned, it's nine months away. Things will change between now and then.

He finished breakfast, washed his dishes, and put them away, while his mom reminisced at the table, changing the facts to suit her new story. They hadn't thrown her to the wolves, innocent and wronged, as she usually said. No, in this version she'd left home and they'd lost touch. The family came out looking better, no longer Evil with a capital *E* but something milder. Bad, maybe. A little Thoughtless.

Her face was flushed and excited. She was describing horses she had ridden, berries she had picked. Jeremy had gotten her hopes way up: the Day of Reconciliation was at hand. Tom made her coffee, extra sweet with half-and-half. He realized then that he felt a bit jealous but relieved. She was pinning her hopes on someone else.

Sooner or later Jeremy would leave and everything would go back to normal. Let Jeremy take the heat for her disappointment this time. Let Jeremy be the one she blamed.

Uncle Richard phoned. "Is your mother home?"

Tom had almost forgotten him, had thought that he'd gotten the message.

"No," Tom lied, as his mother stopped in the bathroom doorway, raising a curious eyebrow. "I don't know where she is."

There was a pause at the other end of the phone. "Tell her I called again."

He hung up and Tom felt vaguely sorry for him.

While his mom took a shower, an aura started as a creeping feeling of dread and quickly advanced until he was sure there was someone in the apartment with them. Someone who wanted to kill them, someone going from room to room with a butcher's knife. It's just the aura, just the aura, he thought. His mom hated being around him when his auras hit. They made her so miserable she went on vacation.

He phoned Mike but Patricia said he was out. He went for a ride to clear his head. He biked down to Stanley Park and along the seawall. The day was sunny and brisk, with a sharp wind blowing in off the ocean. He stopped to watch the boats. Someday he wanted to have enough money to go out on a boat and sail away from everything. They'd lived in BC for eight years and the closest he'd come to getting on a boat was going to North Van on the Seabus.

He almost preferred the seizures to the auras. He never remembered the seizures. There'd be a little blank spot, and then people would be standing over him. Once he'd woken up and some guy was giving him CPR, which fucking hurt because his heart hadn't stopped. Seizures were embarrassing and he woke up sore and tired, but they didn't make him feel this paranoid, like he was the doomed murder victim in the opening sequence of the *X-Files*.

The bike path was crowded as he started off again. Sundays were not the day to go biking at the seawall if you wanted to be alone. He liked the crowds, though, the way that everything seemed so normal. But it was getting cold, the aura was fading, and he was tired. He turned his bike home.

Jeremy wasn't back yet. Mom had left a note on the fridge that she'd been called in, was working the night shift again.

It was her fourth night in a row. He was surprised she was accepting the long hours so placidly but then remembered that she wanted to go back east for Christmas. She'd probably want the extra money.

Tom made himself a sandwich and settled at the kitchen table to do his homework. He'd picked French as his language and was regretting it. Mike said that Spanish was easier and he had some friends who spoke Spanish so he had people to practice on. Tom did his exercises, dutifully conjugating irregular verbs, wishing he'd listened to Mike. Provincials were coming up next year, and if he had any hope of scholarship money, he'd better—

His chair went out from under him and he was on the floor, his head bouncing off the linoleum as he landed sideways, the room going gray for a moment, then blue and gold. He smelled dust before his vision cleared. He thought, This is it, it's over, but the seizure didn't come. He stayed awake with his head throbbing where he'd hit the floor.

"Hi!" Jeremy said cheerfully. "Miss me?"

Jeremy hauled him to his feet, and he swayed, dizzy. He tried to punch Jeremy's arm, missed, and almost fell again, but Jeremy laughed and held him up.

"You goddamn maniac!" he found himself shouting, mad, embarrassed.

"This way," Jeremy said, leading him into the living room by the elbow.

He tried to get his arm out of his cousin's grip, just on the principle of the thing. Jeremy squeezed hard, pain shot up Tom's arm, and he left himself be led.

There were bags in the living room with designer names

on them. God, he thought, where's he getting the money? Jeremy's family was rich, but not that rich.

"Ta-da!" Jeremy said, letting go. He reached down and pulled out a shirt, unfolded it in one broad flap, and held it up for inspection.

"Don't you have enough clothes?" Tom said.

Jeremy rolled his eyes dramatically. "He has eeeyes, but he cannot see. Lord . . ." Jeremy slapped his palm against Tom's forehead. ". . . *Heal* this bliiind soul, that he may finally seeee the light."

"Fuck off," Tom said.

Far from being offended, Jeremy looked more and more benevolent. He said slowly, "Come on, Tommy, take a good look. What size is this shirt? Hmm? Can Tommy tell me that?"

Tom looked at the shirt and saw that there was no way it would fit Jeremy. He looked at the bags around them, the realization slowly dawning that Jeremy was putting him further and further in debt.

"You can take these back," he said sharply. "I won't wear them. I've got clothes."

"And what lovely clothes they are," Jeremy said. "You are truly the epitome of haute couture. Where do you shop? I'm guessing thrift store or garbage can."

Tom looked at him, mute. He turned and left the room, retreating to the bathroom, the only place in the apartment with a decent lock.

He heard the rustle of bags. Jeremy was bringing them into the bedroom. It didn't matter. He'd never wear anything his cousin gave him. Not in a billion years. He heard the closet door squeaking open. Jeremy went into the kitchen. When he came back, Tom heard the hangers clanking. He froze, thinking, No, Jeremy wouldn't do that.

But when he left the bathroom and poked his head into the bedroom, Jeremy was cheerfully dumping Tom's clothes into garbage bags.

Tom charged and caught Jeremy off guard. Jeremy whooped, and they rolled together on the floor. Tom got in three punches before Jeremy pinned him down. Tom was reminded suddenly of Tigger in *Winnie-the-Pooh*. Jeremy wiggled his fingers.

"No!" Tom shouted.

He fought as long as he could, gritting his teeth. Jeremy simply kept tickling him until he gave in, and then he didn't stop until Tom began to cry. Jeremy let him up and told him to sit on the bed. Tom moved automatically. When Jeremy finished dumping the clothes in garbage bags, he lugged them to the bedroom window and tossed them out.

"I saved you a few grungies," he said. "For cleaning and stuff."

Then Jeremy told Tom to go to the kitchen and he went. "You eat?"

"Yes," he said calmly as he could, thinking Jeremy would get bored with the head games if he just didn't react. "Thanks."

"I can make an omelet," Jeremy said.

"I'm fine, thank you."

Jeremy looked puzzled. "You okay, kid?"

"I'm fine, thank you." He picked his French book up off the floor and opened it. "Excuse me. I have homework."

He tried to lose himself in the exercises, but they were boring and he could feel Jeremy wandering around the kitchen watching him. Tom made himself think about scholarships, and that brought him back to what was important. Getting an education. Getting his mom out. Going somewhere.

"You're mad at me." Jeremy sat across from him, eating. "I can tell."

Yeah, and you're psychic, Tom thought. "Would you mind going someplace else?" he said. "I'm busy."

He finished his French homework. When Jeremy pushed back his chair and left the room, Tom moved on to physics. The front door slammed. Tom sat still for a moment, surprised it had worked. He went to the bedroom window to see if his clothes were still on the patchy lawn. Three bags were okay, but the fourth one had burst, dumping his jeans near the bushes. Jeremy appeared. He began to gather the bags. He looked up and saw Tom in the window.

"Catch!" Jeremy said, as he dropped all the bags but one, which he lobbed upwards. It only went as far as the second floor. Jeremy caught it and tossed it up again. The bag still fell short.

"I'll be right down," Tom said.

"Here comes!"

Tom caught it, the plastic ripping in his hands as he scrambled to get the bag inside before it broke.

On the third bag, Mrs. Tupper poked her head out the window and Jeremy almost hit her. She shrieked and pulled back in.

"You stupid kids!" she shouted, shaking her fist at Jeremy. "You goddamn brats! I should call the police on you!"

Jeremy grinned up at her. "Help! Oh, help! I've been beaned by flying garbage!"

"You got no respect! No respect!"

Jeremy did a jig on the lawn. She disappeared back into her apartment and Tom shook his head. Jeremy was picking the jeans off the bushes when Mrs. Tupper nailed him with a wad of coffee grounds.

He looked up, eyes wide with surprise. A rain of orange peels, egg cartons, and TV-dinner trays came at him, and he dodged them, yelling, "Missed me! Missed me! Now you've got to kiss me!"

Infuriated, Mrs. Tupper shouted, "You hooligan!" and the rain of garbage increased with less and less accuracy as Jeremy bobbed and weaved, picking up the last of the jeans and running for cover.

Tom heard Mrs. Tupper shouting at his cousin in the stairwell and Jeremy giving his goofy, slightly deranged whoop. A few minutes later Jeremy staggered up the stairs, laughing so hard he couldn't walk straight. Mrs. Tupper was doggedly chasing him, leaning on both her canes, a last banana peel dangling from her hand.

Jeremy made it to the top of the stairs, then turned around. Mrs. Tupper hit him in the chest with the banana peel, and he hooted as he fell down. Unimpressed, Mrs. Tupper picked up her pace and advanced on him, her left cane raised above her head. She began to smack him with it as soon as he came in range. Jeremy crawled away, gasping for air as he laughed, dropping jeans as he made a slow and unsteady escape.

"Mrs. Tupper," Tom said. "I think that's enough."

"What you need," Mrs. Tupper said, her voice crisp with

indignation, "is a good wupping." She pivoted on her canes to make a dignified retreat.

Jeremy, reduced to giggling, staggered back to pick up the jeans he'd left behind. Tom went out to help him.

"That was," Jeremy said, giggling again. "The slowest chase in history."

Tom took the jeans from Jeremy as his cousin collapsed again, helpless with laughter. Some of the neighbors opened their doors and peeked out.

"It's okay," Tom said.

Jeremy wiped his eyes. He punched Tom's arm as they went into the apartment. "Kid, you've got no sense of humor."

Tom smiled wanly.

"Come on," Jeremy said. "Lighten up. I've got just the trick."

Jeremy went to the bedroom and Tom followed, jeans draped over his arms. Jeremy pulled his suitcase from under the bed and opened it. There was a black garbage bag inside. It crackled as Jeremy opened it. He held up a bag of cocaine.

"Jeez," Tom said, sitting down on his bed.

"It's just coke," Jeremy said, looking at him. "It's not like it's crack or anything."

"You sell it," Tom said, disappointed, realizing where the money was coming from as he looked at the suitcase.

"No, no, no," Jeremy said. "This friend of mine sells it, but he cuts me some pretty good deals because I store the stuff for him. This stuff"— Jeremy lifted up a packet —"isn't top of the line. He gives me samples. As long as I don't dip too deep, that is."

Tom didn't know what to say.

"Hey, I didn't kill anyone for it or anything," his cousin said. "You ever tried this stuff?"

Tom shook his head.

"Well," Jeremy said, hitting him on the knees. "Let's get you toasted, Clark Kent."

It wasn't too hard to give in, since he was curious. Mike wouldn't touch cocaine, wouldn't do anything anymore except pot, saying he'd rather not be that fucked up and stupid. Tom had never done anything heavy, but he hadn't admitted that; he'd faked knowing what Mike was talking about.

What if the coke reacted with his medication? He hadn't had a seizure in four years. He might relapse, he might have some really freaky reaction and end up in the hospital. Or nothing could happen.

Jeremy opened the bag carefully, laid down four lines, and rolled a hundred-dollar bill into a thin tube. He inhaled hard. He handed the tube to Tom, who copied him.

"Nothing's happening," Tom said.

Jeremy shrugged. "Try again."

Tom made it through the second snort. He waited. He felt a bit buzzed but nothing more. So. This was living dangerously. Life in the fast lane. Yee-hah.

Jeremy handed him the tube and he snorted another half a line. "I don't think it's for me."

Jeremy grunted, smiling at nothing. He got up and opened a window.

Tom felt light. He lifted his arm for no reason and found himself staring at his hand. He had no idea how long he held it up. Jeremy started laughing. He was on the bed, jumping up and down. His shadow loomed in the corner and shrank. Tom blinked slowly, his bones melting into the pillows. His lids felt heavy, his legs were sinking, the room was a vortex, and he was sucked down, slowly, Jeremy moving in the air like an excited poodle doing tricks.

"You," Jeremy said when Tom woke up, "are possibly the most boring partier in the entire world."

Tom rolled over, covering his head with the pillow.

"Come on," Jeremy said, yanking the blankets off. "School time, kid."

"God," Tom muttered, "it can't be morning."

Jeremy poked him out of bed, poked him into the kitchen, fed him cereal, and laid out his clothes. Tom, tired and achy, felt like he hadn't slept for weeks. He didn't want to argue, just wanted to be left alone.

"Here," his cousin said, handing him a bottle of Visine. "Make yourself presentable."

The sharp, sweet smell of pot filled the room like a cheap air freshener. The ceiling was covered in a blue haze.

Jeremy herded him into his car and dropped him off at school. Tom planned on skipping gym. He couldn't miss physics or band. He remembered his medication and dug around in his bag until he found it. He'd already missed too much school. The new no-tolerance rules had come into place this month, and he'd be suspended if he missed any more classes. He stepped into the hallway and felt strange, as if people were watching him. He thought it was an aura, but it didn't feel as intense. Mike had said that happened sometimes; when you first tried pot, you got paranoid. Tom wondered if it was the same with coke.

He put his books in his locker. The black-haired girl with the multiple earrings who had the locker beside him stopped dead when she saw him, open-mouthed. He tried to convince himself that he was imagining it, but she turned to watch him leave, still looking shocked.

It's okay, he told himself. Keep calm. Don't look stoned.

He walked to his physics class, telling himself that conversations were not going quiet as he passed. He fixed his gaze straight ahead, determined to appear sober.

The buzzer rang, and he jumped at the loudness of it. He was late. Maybe he should just skip classes altogether. No, he decided, go ahead. He pushed the classroom door open. Mr. Calloway's voice droned through the air, low and monotone, telling everyone to open their books to page 143. Tom took his place at the back of the class, feeling eyes on him. His neighbor snickered.

"Hey," the guy said loudly. "It's Mr. Armani."

Tom sat still, not comprehending.

"Whoa, check out the duds," someone else said, and the class turned to stare at him.

Tom looked down. Jeremy had put him in some kind of suit and he hadn't noticed, he'd been that stoned. Hadn't really cared what he put on, never really saw what he put on until now, when he was being gaped at like a freak.

Mr. Calloway tapped the desk to get everyone's attention, then began to write equations on the board. Interest in Tom faded as Mr. Calloway made his way through the lesson.

In the bathroom after class, Tom checked himself in the mirror. He'd forgotten the haircut too. He looked goofy. He didn't mind being laughed at wearing his normal clothes; he could handle it then, shrug it off. But now it was different. Everyone would think he was trying to be cool.

I am going to kill Jeremy, he thought. I am going to strangle him while he sleeps.

The buzzer rang. He didn't want to leave the bathroom. He felt embarrassed about being embarrassed, told himself he didn't care what anyone thought.

Fuck it. He moved down the hallway, opened the locker, manhandled his bassoon out, and made his way to band, sober and tense.

The reaction in band was more dramatic than in physics. Jaws dropped as he sat, careful not to meet anyone's eyes. The French horn player sitting beside him burst out laughing. Tom opened the bassoon case, concentrating firmly on keeping a deadpan expression.

He knew Paulina Mazenkowski had turned around. He didn't want to see her giggling.

"Hey, Tom," she said.

As calmly as he could, he looked at her.

"You clean up nice," she said, smiling right at him before she turned back and they started warm-up scales.

She smiled at him again, before she left with her friends,

but he couldn't quite manage to smile back, so he nodded, feeling like an idiot, like the biggest phony on the face of the earth.

"Holy fucking Jesus!" Mike said, when they met in the hallway. "What the fuck happened to you?"

Tom sat down, tired. "I got a haircut."

"Shit," Mike said. "Man, you look like a fucking retard."

"Thanks."

"I mean it. You look like a goddamn suit. What happened to you, man? Where'd your brain go?"

"It's *hair*," Tom said. "Not a face-lift."

"You sold out," Mike said. "You bought into it. You're a fucking clone."

Tom pulled out his sandwich and began to eat. He didn't feel up to dealing with Mike. What was the big problem? He'd always been scummy and Mike had never cared. Tom looked up and Mike was gone. Just like that.

He couldn't take it anymore and skipped the afternoon. The whole day, he decided, was just too weird.

Tom woke up on the couch. The phone rang and kept ringing, and he reached for it, bleary-eyed. " 'Lo?"

"Tom. I want to talk to your mother. Now."

"Who's 'is?" He groped for the clock, then remembered it was in the kitchen.

"You goddamn well know who it is," the man said, and Tom realized it was Uncle Richard, sounding more pissed off than usual. "Where is she?"

"I dunno," Tom said. "Wait. Lemme check the fridge."

He put the phone down and stumbled into the kitchen. There was nothing where Mom usually left messages. He went back to the living room and picked up the phone, but Uncle Richard had hung up. Poor bastard, Tom thought.

He sat for a few moments, then went to his bedroom to change. He couldn't find his real clothes, his jeans and T-shirts. He was hunting under the bed when Jeremy came in.

"Hey, Sleeping Beauty," he said, kicking Tom in the butt. "About time you woke up. Where's Aunt Chrissy?"

"Where's my clothes?" Tom said. He pushed himself up onto his knees.

"I asked first." Jeremy crossed his arms over his chest. "Where is she?"

"I don't know. I want my clothes back." Tom felt himself getting angry and breathed deeply. A sudden suspicion made him dizzy. "You threw them out. You—"

"Relax, relax. I'm keeping them over at a friend's place. You can have them back when you earn them."

"Earn them?" He stood up. "Those are my clothes! I bought them! You—"

"*Meep*," Jeremy said, wiggling his fingers.

There was nothing he could say to that.

"Smart boy," Jeremy said. "You hungry?"

Jeremy disappeared into the kitchen and made some Kraft dinner. Tom could smell it cooking and came to the table as Jeremy put the pot on the table. Tom ate two helpings. He couldn't remember macaroni and cheese tasting so good. He made himself a sandwich afterward, then scooped some ice cream.

Jeremy picked at his food. His left foot tapped against the

floor. Tom watched him. A thin trickle of blood leaked out of Jeremy's right nostril and dribbled down his face. Before it dropped onto the plate, the blood quivered on his chin. Jeremy noticed Tom staring at him and looked down as if to check his fly.

"Fuck," Jeremy said. He wiped his nose with the back of his hand, smearing blood across his cheek.

His cousin left the kitchen. Tom heard the bathroom faucet running. He got up and scraped Jeremy's dinner into the garbage. The TV suddenly blared to life and the lounger squealed as Jeremy plopped down in the living room.

The feeling that something was not right was getting stronger. It's an aura, Tom thought. It's from hitting my head the other night. He should get up and leave, he thought, sneak out, go to Mike's place, hang out for a few days, borrow some clothes. Or he could stay and put up with the shit Jeremy was handing out. Or he could tell Mom that Jeremy was a drug pusher. She'd never stand for that, too afraid that Tom was going to become an addict and run away, disappear, then reappear dead. She'd seen it happen to her friends' kids.

Option one, going over to Mike's place, had the disadvantage of being unreliable. Mike might not be home, or might not be his friend anymore, after today. It bugged him that Mike could be so superficial.

Then there were the bills. In spite of everything, Jeremy had paid off the electric bill, had shown him the receipt. Tom had checked it out himself, privately, and discovered that Jeremy was telling the truth. They were all paid up. Jeremy had tacked the phone bill up on the wall of their bedroom and circled how much they owed. If he screwed up with Jeremy, the chances that his cousin would pay off the bills were very, very small.

So. He'd stick it out. He'd get laughed at and bossed around. Big deal. How long could it last? A month? Two months? Only he hated it. He didn't know if he could face another day of being stared at. Time to talk to his cousin.

He took a deep breath, then another. He went into the living room, where his cousin was zoning out in front of MuchMusic.

"Could you turn it down?" Tom said.

Jeremy shook his head.

"I got to talk to you!"

"Later!" Jeremy shouted back, eyes narrowed to slits, not looking at him.

Tom stayed for a few more minutes, then left, disgusted.

He searched his bedroom, his mother's bedroom, the hallway closet, and the bathroom but couldn't find his clothes. The stuff hanging up in his own closet made him cringe. Nerdball stuff.

The bedroom door opened and he expected to see Jeremy. He was surprised to see Uncle Richard and then completely surprised when Uncle Richard's fist connected with his jaw. He hit the wall and Uncle Richard grabbed his shirt, held him up by it.

"Where is she?" Uncle Richard said, his voice completely calm.

"I nono," Tom said, his mouth not working properly.

Uncle Richard pushed his face right up against Tom's, his

flat black eyes wide and blank. "You're lying," Richard said.

"No, twuth."

Tom saw the fist coming this time and put his arms up. The fist hit the wall beside him and he heard the plaster give.

"I can hurt you," Uncle Richard said. He pulled his fist back. "Don't lie to me anymore. I don't like it."

Unsteadily, Uncle Richard reached to pull him close, grabbing a fistful of shirt. Tom kicked out, getting him in the shins, and Uncle Richard's face distorted. But even shocked and in pain, Uncle Richard kept his grip. Tom tried to bite his hands, tried to force them off, but he couldn't get out of Uncle Richard's stranglehold. Tom went for the groin, tried poking him in the eyes, while Richard slammed him against the wall, pulled him up, slammed him again.

Then Uncle Richard was collapsing, dragging him down, and Jeremy was standing over them with a baseball bat. Uncle Richard let him go and charged Jeremy, who swung and connected with Uncle Richard's shoulder. Jeremy popped him in the temple next and he went down. Jeremy prodded him in the side. When Uncle Richard didn't move, he raised the bat and brought it down on the man's right knee, then on his left. He hit him in the sides, paused, hit him on the shoulders. Tom could hear the dull thunk of a bone cracking.

"S'nough," Tom said, when Jeremy raised the bat again.

Jeremy paused, then hit Uncle Richard in the groin. Uncle Richard didn't move and Tom was afraid he was dead.

Jeremy came over and helped him up carefully.

"S'nough," Tom said.

"I heard you, you moron," Jeremy said. He set Tom

down on the bed. "When he comes back here and beats the crap out of you, you remember that you're the one who stopped me."

"Call amb'lance. 'S hurt."

"Yes, he is," Jeremy said. "How'd he get in?"

" 'S got a key."

"She let him have a key? How many other guys have keys?" Tom didn't like what he was implying. "Jus' him."

"Are you sure?"

Tom glared at him. Jeremy got up and searched through Uncle Richard's clothes until he found the key, which he pocketed before he took Uncle Richard by the ankles and dragged him from the room.

Tom came to, not knowing when or where he'd passed out, struggling against the seat belt before Jeremy said, "Don't bleed on the seat! Jesus, here!" He handed him a rag. "Hold it over your lip!"

He had a vague impression of the drive, then of a waiting room and a nurse handing him a lemon-scented napkin, the kind that Kentucky Fried Chicken gave out. As he sat, leaning against Jeremy, his muscles hurt in a familiar way. Before he'd gone on medication, he used to wake up like this a lot. He didn't really mind the seizures. They were over in five, maybe ten minutes and he didn't remember them. It was when he woke up and people's attitudes about him had changed—they tiptoed around him, spoke to him as if he couldn't understand them, or just avoided him altogether.

Leaning against Jeremy wasn't comfortable and he was

tired. He curled up on the waiting-room couch and closed his eyes.

" . . . despite the blows to his head, nothing's showing up on the X ray," a woman's voice said, as he surfaced again. "We'd like to keep him here a few days, just to be on the safe side. Do you have his Carecard?"

"No," Jeremy said. "I can pay cash."

"Uncle," Tom said. "Richard."

Jeremy and the woman in a white lab coat stared at him.

"Hello," the woman said. He recognized her, one of the doctors who'd done tests on him before. Dr. Ahava leaned over him and shone a flashlight in his eyes. "How you feeling, Tom?"

"Hiya, space cadet," Jeremy said at the same time. "Welcome back to planet Earth."

"He okay?"

"Who?" Jeremy said.

He focused again. "Richard."

"Yeah, he's still breathing," Jeremy said. He turned to the woman. "Guy who punched him out. Mother's boyfriend."

Dr. Ahava tsk-tsked. She tested his ribs gently. "How hard did he hit you, Tom?"

"Not too hard."

"Hmmm. How long after he hit you did you have the seizure?"

"Seizure?" Tom said, puzzled. "I didn't have a seizure."

"About ten, maybe fifteen minutes," Jeremy said.

"He's lying," Tom said. "I'm fine. I've got a headache, that's all."

"Tom," she said, patiently. "This is very important. I need you to tell me the truth. Have you had any other seizures lately?"

"No. Just some bad auras."

"Are you sure?"

"Yes, I'm sure."

"You wouldn't lie to me?"

"No. I didn't have a seizure. I'm sure of it."

Dr. Ahava exchanged knowing looks with Jeremy. Tom's eyes began to droop. He was so tired, could feel himself falling asleep. He was sore, too, just like . . . after a seizure. Christ. She asked him more questions and he thought he answered them but couldn't be sure.

"You listen to your cousin," she said before she left. "Press charges. You shouldn't let him get away with this."

Then Jeremy lowered the bed so he was lying flat. Someone on the other side of the curtain was snoring. The walls were a shade of green that he found nauseating. Here he was. Back in the hospital. His favorite place in the whole fucking world.

"We'll go to the police station when you get out," Jeremy said.

Tom shook his head. "Won't."

Jeremy looked stubborn. "We'll talk about it tomorrow."

Tom closed his eyes, refusing to be drawn in. He heard Jeremy get up. The swinging overhead lamp snapped off. As he was going under, he heard Jeremy say, "You moron."

■■

"You've missed your last three appointments," Dr. Ahava started off saying when she came and sat by his bed after he finished his breakfast.

"I've still got enough stuff." Tom crossed his arms over his chest. "I haven't had a seizure in four years."

"You had one last night," Dr. Ahava said. Her eyes bored into him. She had sharp gray eyes that were perfect for boring.

"Nothing happened. I'm perfectly all right."

"Tom," she said. "You had a seizure. Your cousin saw it. Why would he lie?"

"Because he's a prick," Tom said.

Dr. Ahava made a note, scribbling something long and damning. He felt his heart picking up speed, thinking of foster homes and hospitals and all the things the doctor could convince his mother to do.

"Tom, I'm going to ask you again." She put aside her pen and clipboard. "Did you have a seizure?"

"Maybe."

She leaned forward. "What?"

He sighed, then repeated it louder.

Dr. Ahava nodded. "Look, I have no idea what caused a seizure after so long without an incident. Maybe your medicine is inadequate or your body chemistry is changing. Maybe it was just the blow to your head. Maybe it's something more serious. We simply won't know unless we do some more tests."

"Yeah, I know the routine."

"If you want your seizures back under control," Dr. Ahava said, "you have to cooperate."

"I know. I will. I am."

"Good," she said, suddenly energetic. "Let's get cracking."

His mother came in the afternoon and caught him napping. He hated it when people watched him sleep.

"You okay, Tommy?"

He sat up. "Yeah. Everyone's just making a big deal out of nothing. I'm fine, really. I'm just tired."

Tears leaked down her face as she touched his fat lip. "It looks real bad, Tommy."

He flinched. "Looks worse than it is."

"I'm so sorry. I am. I really am."

"It's not your fault. It's not even Richard's fault. Look, I'm okay."

"Jeremy says . . . " She stopped.

"What?"

"He says . . . it happened."

Oh, fuck, Tom thought. "Just a little one."

"Oh," she said, not looking at him. "Well. Well. I brought you some pajamas. Mrs. Tupper baked some cookies for you. Mike called." She wiped her nose and smiled. "Jeremy's taking me to *Kiss of the Spider Woman*! Can you imagine?" She giggled. "Me, all dressed up and going to a musical."

"When?"

"Next week." Her eyes were bright as she talked. He didn't remember falling asleep, but when he woke up she was gone.

..

The day they checked out of the hospital Dr. Ahava said, "I've talked to your cousin. He said he's watching you while your mother works. Is that true?"

Tom turned to Jeremy, who was looking very earnest. Jeremy winked at him.

"Yes," Tom said faintly.

Dr. Ahava looked satisfied. "Good. He can drive you to your next appointment this Friday. I will see you here, won't I? Four o'clock sharp?"

"Yes."

Dr. Ahava shook hands with Jeremy. "Good meeting you. See that he doesn't forget."

His cousin rocked on his heels. "I'll do my best."

Jeremy drove him home. Tom collapsed on the couch. His cousin went out and came back.

"She's still not home," he said.

Tom opened one eye. "Must be working."

Jeremy grunted. "If she worked as much as you say she does you guys wouldn't be so deep in the hole, would you?"

Tom put his arm over his eyes and ignored him.

When he woke, the apartment was still. He was hungry but didn't want to move. Jeremy, he saw, had left some chocolate pudding on the coffee table.

His lip was still twice its normal size and the bruise that surrounded it was dark purple with green edges. There was a cut near the center that hurt whenever he closed his mouth. He hadn't wanted to go to school but Jeremy had pronounced him fit and that had been that.

He was glad when the buzzer rang for math and glad that there wasn't any band today, not that he could play. The last person he wanted to see right now was Paulina. He wasn't used to his clothes; he hated being a freak.

His mom had been gone for three days. The laundry plant had called and left a message on their machine saying they needed her tonight, could she make it in? He wondered if Uncle Richard had gotten to her after Jeremy pounded him. He kept seeing her dead. He was tired and couldn't focus; his nerves felt raw.

Jeremy hadn't let him go back to sleep the night before. Tom had woken up and it had been dark except for sudden blinding flashes. Jeremy was taking pictures.

Tom had held his hands in front of his eyes. "What the hell—"

"Evidence," Jeremy had said. "When we catch old Ricky, your bruises will probably be gone."

"I'm not pressing charges! Fuck! How many times do I have to tell you? It's all right. We're even!"

"You forgive him? He punches you around and you forgive him? You stupid little moron. That's what's going to get you killed."

They'd argued about it for a long time. He wouldn't give in. Mom'd be upset, think it was her fault, and leave. He knew she would, and then he'd have to run away. He hated foster homes, hated being someone's charity case, hated having to be grateful all the time. Jeremy might stick around for a while, but Tom didn't know how much longer he could put up with him.

When the buzzer rang, Tom jumped in his seat. The class felt like it had just started. The drugs were making him spacey. He followed the others out of the classroom and walked straight into Paulina.

"Hi," she said, staring at his lip.

"Hi," he said, his hands trying to find pockets. He wasn't wearing jeans though, and the pants he had on didn't have any pockets.

"Someone must really love you," she said, fascinated by his bruise. "Does it hurt?"

"Only when I laugh," he said.

She smiled. She had a beautiful smile, all teeth and cotton-candy pink lips. "Where's your brother?"

Tom blinked. "Who?"

"Jeremy, you nerd," she said, nudging him.

"He's my cousin," Tom said. "He's not my brother."

She looked confused. "That's not what he says."

That liar. "Yeah, well, Jeremy exaggerates sometimes."

Paulina hugged herself. "I think it's sweet. Him acting like your big brother. You're so lucky. Tell him I can't make it tonight, but I'll see him tomorrow at the same place."

"You're . . . seeing Jeremy?"

She winked. "If he behaves himself. Bye!" She pecked his cheek.

He leaned against the locker to stop himself from falling over. Jeremy knew. And Jeremy didn't give a damn. Tom closed his eyes. Jeremy was older, good-looking, and rich. If

I was Paulina, he thought, who would I see? Jeremy or a nerdy grade ten guy.

"Yes?" Patricia said, opening the door slightly.

"Is Mike home?" Tom said.

"Mike? Who—" She stopped, squinted, closed the door. He could hear her taking off the chain. The door opened again and Patricia came forward. "Tom?"

He nodded.

"Tom? Oh, my God, I can't believe it!" she said, laughing.

Tom instantly regretted coming to Mike's house, wished he'd gone straight home.

Patricia pulled him in, reached out, and touched his hair, amazed. "You look—"

"Goofy, I know," he said.

"No, no, no," she said, grabbing his shoulders and holding him out for inspection. "You look like a gentleman. Well. Except for the fat lip. My God. I thought you were a salesman or one of those Jehovah's Witnesses. Tom. I can't believe it's you. Mike! Tom's here! Evan, come see this!"

Great. Tom, the traveling freak show, he thought as she waited for him to take off his shoes before she let him into the kitchen. Mike sat at the table, pretending to gag as she exclaimed over his matching socks.

Mike's uncle Evan came in the kitchen looking distracted. He stopped when he saw Tom. "Hoo-yah!" he said, and Tom wished more than ever that he'd gone home.

Mike kicked the kitchen table.

With Patricia and Evan there, it was hard to ask Mike what

the fuck was the matter with him, so instead he said, "Didn't see you at lunch today."

Mike's eyes wandered around the room, looking at everything except Tom.

Patricia and Evan exchanged glances, then excused themselves. Mike walked over to the refrigerator. "You want some pizza?"

Tom shrugged. "Sure."

"It's vegetarian."

"That's okay."

"It's shitty."

Tom took a deep breath. "Can I crash here tonight?"

Mike pulled the pizza out of the refrigerator and put it in the microwave. "I dunno."

For a long time the only sound was the hum of the microwave. Tom got up and walked out of the kitchen. As he left, the microwave beeped. No one was in the living room. He was glad. He put his shoes back on. When he was halfway down the driveway, Patricia yelled, "Aren't you staying for dinner?"

He shook his head and waved good-bye. She raised her hand, waved once, then closed the door.

He ended up in the park, sitting on the swings, dragging his feet in the sand. The sky was clear as the sun set. The streetlights flickered on.

Mike had brought him to a hostel once. It cost nine bucks a night. The mattress was thin and the blankets were rattylooking. The walls were covered with graffiti. He picked at his suit. He was probably overdressed.

So. Mike, who'd never been bothered by his seizures or his grunge look or his mooching, freaked because he looked like a suit.

And Paulina liked Jeremy.

He could understand it. Hell, who was he kidding? He'd never had a chance with Paulina. At least Jeremy hadn't rubbed it in, hadn't said, Hey, guess who I'm seeing tonight?

He didn't want to deal with Jeremy, who had become so crazed about Tom's taking his medicine that he watched him down every pill.

It got cold and he went home. The lights in the apartment were on. He stopped, not wanting to go up. He was taking out his keys when he heard Mike say, "Where the fuck you been?"

Tom had thought he was beyond being surprised. "Hey."

"Hey yourself," Mike said.

"Patricia know where you are?"

Mike grinned, ducking his head. "We had a discussion."

"Yeah? You break any windows this time?"

"Nah. Just a couple of dishes. It safe to go up?"

To the apartment, he meant. Tom didn't know how to answer that one.

"You want to talk about it?" Mike said.

Tom shook his head. "No."

Mike looked suddenly relieved. "Good."

They went to a party but it was a bust. The host was drunk enough to think he was a good guitar player. He knew about three chords and mixed them up. Everyone had escaped to the kitchen except for three or four people passed out on the living room floor.

"Oooooh," the man sang. "There's . . . " He struck an unidentifiable chord. "A Baa . . ." Chord. "Baaad . . ."

Mike, fingers in his ears, got up and left the room.

Tom spaced out on the couch for a while before Mike came back and got him up.

They goofed around outside for a while after that. Someone had left a Nerf hockey set on the sidewalk, probably little kids because the shoulderpads were tiny. The helmets didn't fit the two of them, but they tied them on anyway and played. They clutched their sides and feigned violent death when the Nerfball hit them.

Back at Mike's place, Tom fell asleep on the rock-hard futon while Mike played video games, quietly swearing at the TV screen.

Thursday morning started with Evan stomping downstairs, dragging Mike off the floor by his ear and screaming at him for leaving the house when he was grounded. They ate breakfast in sullen silence. Patricia drove them to school, her eyes straight ahead. The only sounds were the car and the syrupy cheerfulness of Patricia's favorite soft-rock station.

"Tom," Patricia said when she stopped the car. "I'd appreciate it if you stayed away from our house for a while. Mike's not going to have any visitors for a few weeks."

Tom got out of the car without answering. Patricia grabbed Mike's sleeve. "Don't plan on going anywhere for a long time, because you are so grounded—"

Mike jerked away, then slammed the door on the rest of what she was saying. She glared for a moment but took off.

Mike rolled his eyes.

"Later," Tom said to Mike.

He made it to all his classes except band. The idea of seeing Paulina made him cringe.

When he got home Tom couldn't find his medicine. He opened the bathroom cabinet and the bottle was gone. He tried to remember if he'd moved it. He searched his room, thinking maybe he'd just put it down somewhere and forgotten. He ransacked the kitchen, opened the fridge, opened every cabinet.

Jeremy wouldn't do that, he thought. Jeremy fucking pushes them down my throat. He wouldn't hide them.

After going through the living room and bedroom one more time, he knew. Goddamn him.

He could go one, maybe two days without it. Then all that would happen was a few seizures. Nothing drastic. He could go get the prescription refilled. Say he dumped them down the sink by accident.

Tom stopped pacing. He went back to his bedroom, pulled out Jeremy's suitcase, and opened it. The coke was still there. He weighed it in his hand and smiled.

Two can play that game.

Jeremy was waiting for him in the living room when he got home from school the next day. They looked at each other for a long time, neither saying anything.

"Hello, stranger," Jeremy finally said.

"Jeremy," Tom said.

"Come on in. Have a seat."

"You have something that belongs to me," Tom said.

Jeremy held up the bottle. "I was looking for you the other night. Remember our deal. You're supposed to tell me when you're staying out."

"Yeah?" Tom said.

"Yeah," Jeremy said. "I was worried. Thought maybe Richard got to you."

"So you hid my medicine."

He tilted his head. "Seemed like a good idea at the time. I think you have something of mine too."

Tom tensed. "I do."

Jeremy nodded, still grinning. "Didn't think you had it in you."

"I want my medicine back."

Jeremy flipped the bottle to him. Tom caught it. He expected Jeremy to dive across the coffee table or something. "And I want you to stop treating me like I'm six years old."

"You are treated the way you act," Jeremy said smugly.

"Then you should be locked up in a loony bin."

"Where's my coke?"

Tom hesitated. "I taped it to the bottom of your car."

Jeremy whooped. Tom hadn't expected him to be amused. He had been dreading this moment but Jeremy only laughed.

Just when Tom thought it was going to be okay, Jeremy lunged and Tom scrambled back, thinking that his cousin was going to punch him. But Jeremy plugged his nose with one hand and covered his mouth with the other, leaning into him so that Tom fell back onto the couch. As suddenly as he'd attacked, Jeremy let go, laughing as if it was all in good fun.

"Don't ever do anything like that again." Jeremy slapped him lightly.

He stood, brushed himself off. "Now," he said cheerfully, "better get your homework done before we see your lady doc."

Jeremy drove him to the hospital, sat outside in the waiting room, chatted with Dr. Ahava, then drove Tom home.

"You can go out," he told Tom, just before he took off. "But you'd better be back for dinner or you're dead meat."

Tom stood on the corner watching Jeremy's car squeal down the street. Just my luck. The only person who really gives a shit if I live or die is a whacked-out drug addict who likes playing God.

Third Contact

"Tommy!" his mom said, when he came in. She threw her arms around him, then brought him into the living room. He sucked in a breath, forced it out.

"Isn't it gorgeous!" she said. "I couldn't *believe* it when the delivery men came! I thought they were at the wrong door. Oh, Tom, isn't it just marvelous?"

His heart beat too fast as he stared at the large-screen TV and the surround-sound system on the brand-new entertainment center. He couldn't even guess how much it had all cost. He wanted to trust Jeremy. He wanted to believe in him. But somehow, some way, Jeremy was going to make them pay for it.

"Mom," he said.

She turned to him, and he knew what he had to do. Her smile faded. She was happy and he was going to make her unhappy.

He pulled the suitcase out from under Jeremy's bed. He opened the lid and picked up the black garbage bag filled with coke. Her eyes went dead and blank.

She said she hadn't really believed their luck either.

Once she made up her mind she moved fast. She collected Jeremy's things and set them in the hallway. She even packed up the entertainment center.

"You've got to give the clothes back," she said.

"Can I keep some?"

"No," she said, her face cold.

He shifted uncomfortably.

"It's blood money, honey," she said. "Only bad can come from it."

"But he took my clothes. I'll give them back when I—"

She stopped packing. "He what?"

"He's got my clothes. You think I'm wearing this by choice?" Tom gestured at his suit jacket. He smiled. "This practically screams 'Mug me.' "

When she didn't laugh, he said, "I'll give them back."

"Why didn't you tell me?" she said flatly.

He didn't know what to say. Her lip began to quiver the way it did before she cried.

"I want you to go over to Mike's," she said.

Tom was shocked. She hated Mike. "Why?"

"This is between me and him. I don't want you here."

"But—"

"Tommy," she said, putting her hands to her temples. "Don't argue with me. Please." Not looking at him, she asked, "Was it really Richard?"

"What?" he said.

"Or was it Jeremy?"

"I don't understand."

"If you're protecting him, you don't have to. I know he has a temper. I know he's family, but if he's hitting you, you can tell me."

He considered lying. No. He didn't need to. "He's not."

She sighed, long and slow. "He told me it was an inheritance," she said. "Can you believe it? I did."

The mood at Mike's was grim. Mike had locked himself in his bedroom and wouldn't come out. He was playing his stereo loud. Nirvana rang through the house. His aunt and uncle looked disgusted. Tom stayed for a while, then said good-bye, glad to be out of there.

He waited a few hours in the park before he went home. When he opened the door, the first thing he noticed was that all Jeremy's things were missing from the hallway. He put his bike into the closet. The foldaway bed was back in its corner. He walked down the hallway. His bedroom looked empty, bigger without Jeremy's things taking up space.

His mom was standing by the window. She came up to him and put an arm around his waist.

"Well," she said. "That's that."

"I'm surprised you let him stay in the first place."

"He's family, Tommy."

"Aunt Rhoda told me why he got kicked out of military school." He hated lying to her, but it was the only way he was ever going to find out what had happened.

She took her arm away. "He didn't mean to go that far. It was self-defense."

Tom forced himself to keep his expression neutral. "Not the way Aunt Rhoda tells it."

"Hmph," she said. "That old bat never liked Jeremy. Don't listen to a word she says. They would never have acquitted him if he'd been guilty. He was such a sweet boy. Always so helpful. A little gentleman." She brought his hands to her cheek and started to cry. Tom saw that she was getting really upset. She didn't look like she could take much more.

Her symptoms started as the week wore on. By Friday, he knew she'd been dry as long as she could. She fidgeted. She scrubbed a part of the kitchen floor, stopped, and then started to reorganize the kitchen. She sat down, her foot tapping rapidly. She wanted to leave but needed an excuse. He couldn't do anything right when she got to this stage. He disappeared into the bedroom and sat on his bed, his homework spread around him.

She stopped in at his bedroom and leaned on the door frame. "He gave his keys back. You don't have to worry."

"Yeah," he said.

"I'll see you in a while."

"Night," he said.

She lingered for a moment. "Take care."

He listened for the sound of the front door closing. Perversely, he found he missed Jeremy now that he was gone. I did the right thing, he told himself.

But he doubted it now, when it was dark and the apartment was empty.

She didn't come back that night. He considered going downtown but he hated cruising the skid bars, and even if he found her it would just embarrass them both. The best thing to do was leave her alone. He had a sudden flash that she probably felt smothered by him, the way he had with Jeremy. Her life, he thought. Don't bug her.

He moved into the living room and watched TV. As he was drifting off to sleep, he realized that the band was in Bellingham this weekend. After all that, Jeremy hadn't loaned him the money to go on the trip. He yawned. He wondered if Jeremy had paid the phone bill. Didn't seem likely. The weatherman said it was going to rain tonight and tomorrow until the afternoon. He hoped she had an umbrella. He kept his eyes open until they burned and the TV blurred. Canned laughter from an old sitcom filled the living room.

The lounger squeaked. Tom woke slowly, sensing someone else in the living room, thinking, She's back.

He turned his head, slitting his eyes open.

"Hiya kid," Jeremy said.

Tom, instantly awake, fumbled to sit up.

"Take it easy," Jeremy said. "Just dropping your stuff off."

Tom saw the five garbage bags around the sofa. He slumped back. His cousin had brought him his clothes. He hadn't thought he would. He felt a reflex guilt, then a flutter of panic. Jeremy was here. He wasn't supposed to be. "Jeez."

"Scared you, huh?" Jeremy started channel surfing. "Your security system sucks. You need a dead bolt."

"What are you doing here?"

"Thought we needed to talk."

"About what?"

Jeremy's face lightened in amusement. "Oh, I don't know. The plight of the Amazon rain forest. The possibility of starting a colony on Mars. Maybe some golf tips. Should I use wood or aluminum clubs to get out of a sand trap?"

The TV burst into a jingle for a brand of toothpaste. Jeremy hunted for the remote. He turned the set off and the living room went black. The silence stretched.

"Guess I came down heavy on you, huh?"

Tom's eyes adjusted to the dark. Jeremy had leaned his head so far back on the lounger that he was facing the ceiling.

"You could say that," Tom said.

"You should have said something," Jeremy said. "Instead of lying to your mother."

"I didn't," Tom said.

"You think I'm a pusher?"

"Aren't you?"

Jeremy laughed. "Kid . . . " he started. His hand moved to his shirt pocket. His lighter flared to life. He lit a cigarette. "Fuck. What a life."

"Where're you getting all your money then? Tell me that. You don't even have a job."

"I got clients calling me all day, twenty-four hours a day. You've seen them, haven't you? I've got cops following me, and I spend my money like it's going out of style. Yeah, I'm a drug dealer. A really smart one too." After another long silence Jeremy said, "For fuck's sake, kid, I'm being sarcastic."

Tom felt the beginnings of a headache. "I know."

Jeremy turned the TV back on. In the flickering light he looked tired. Tom lay back on the couch. He put his arm over his eyes. The possibility that Jeremy was okay crossed his mind. He put it down to being tired.

"My dad's dad died. He hated everyone except me. He had a lot of money. He left me everything. End of story," Jeremy said.

"How'd he get his money?"

Jeremy looked disgusted. "Aluminum. He bought aluminum shares during World War II. My blood type is A negative. Anything else?"

"Why'd he give it to you?"

"How am I supposed to know?"

Tom narrowed his eyes.

"I was in his old regiment," Jeremy said slowly, through gritted teeth. "And everyone thought I'd go far."

Tom said, "So?"

Jeremy stood up and saluted. "There has always been a Rieger in the army, ever since the plains of Abraham. And by God, there will always be a Rieger in the army."

Jeremy sat down, looking moody and pissed. Tom wanted to ask more questions but thought he'd wait until Jeremy was less strung out.

Tom heard the telltale snore and turned his head. Sure enough, his cousin was out. He thought of what his mother would say if she came through the door and saw Jeremy sleeping there.

But she's not here, is she? a part of his mind said.

He was tired of thinking. There was a strange comfort in Jeremy's snoring. He'd gotten used to it. It was easy to slide into sleep hearing that.

Tom woke up first. Jeremy had made his way to the bedroom sometime during the night and was sprawled over the bed. Tom carefully picked up Jeremy's jeans and jacket and went through them.

Jeremy had some keys, his wallet, a comb, and a pocket-sized computer organizer. Tom glanced at Jeremy, still dead to the world. Tom opened the wallet. It had Jeremy's driver's license and a bank-machine receipt between two fifties. Jeremy had taken out $460.00 the night before. The balance in his account was $127,894.73.

Tom put the slip back in the wallet, then the wallet back in the pants. So he's not a millionaire. He was blowing his money and it was going to run out. That made Tom feel better. Still, $127,000. He couldn't imagine having that much money. If he had it he sure wouldn't blow it.

Jeremy shifted, and Tom waited. But his cousin stayed asleep.

Maybe he hadn't seen the figure right. Maybe it was $2,700. He knew he was just being nosy now. He knew that if he was caught he was going to be in trouble, but his fingers itched to take the wallet out and look at it again. He found himself doing it, watching Jeremy carefully.

The wallet was thin. Jeremy had a membership at Movie

Madness, a library card from Metro Toronto Public Library, and a photo of some kid that Tom slowly realized was him.

He pulled it out. He didn't remember it being taken. He was sitting in front of a birthday cake with eight candles. On the back, in his mother's writing, "Hi Jeremy! We're doing well. Vancouver is nice. All my love, Aunt Christa."

He put the picture back in place and slipped the wallet into one of the pockets. In his haste to get out of there, he forgot which one he'd taken it from.

Tom went to the kitchen. When Jeremy came in and sat across from him a few minutes later, he knew that Jeremy had been faking sleep. He'd known that Tom was going through his wallet and had let him do it.

"I've got letters too," Jeremy said. "You want to see them?" With a malicious smile he said, "Or should I leave them in my wallet?"

Tom's face went red; he felt the flush spreading but couldn't stop it. He couldn't look at his cousin anymore. He stared at his hands.

"You could just ask me," Jeremy said. "Wait."

He left the kitchen and came back with a pen. He drew something on his fingers and Tom leaned toward him to see what it was. It was faces. Jeremy held up his left hand. He'd given the index finger an extra large blue mouth. No, a bruised mouth.

" 'Jeremy,' " Jeremy said in a high squeaky voice, " 'what the fuck do you want?' " He held up his right hand. "Well, kid. I'm here to rob you of all your worldly possessions, kill you, and inherit your vast fortune. 'But I don't have a vast fortune, Jeremy!' Whoops! Wrong kid."

Tom found himself laughing. "You are truly strange."

" 'Come on, Jeremy. Be serious. What are you doing here?' I'm family, kid. Isn't that enough?" The finger-Tom picked up the pen and bonked the finger-Jeremy over the head. " 'Get real! Like I'm going to believe that!' " Jeremy looked up. He moved his finger people in front of his face. "I want to help."

"Why?" Tom said.

"When we were kids you thought I was your brother." Jeremy wiped his hands on the table and the finger puppets smeared across the surface.

"Right," Tom said, snorting.

"It's true."

Jeremy looked down at his fingers. "Your mom wrote me all the time. She was always bragging what a good kid you were. Did you know that? I can show you the letters."

For once, Jeremy looked completely serious. "No. It's okay."

Jeremy didn't smile. "Is it?"

"Yeah," Tom said. "It is."

Jeremy dropped him off at Mike's. Tom didn't feel like spending the day with his cousin. He told Jeremy he was going over to Mike's to study. Mike was in the backyard shooting hoops. He stopped and stared at the car. He whistled.

Jeremy said, "I'll pick you up later."

"I know how to get home," Tom said. "Hey, Mike. This is my cousin Jeremy. Jeremy, this is Mike McConnell."

Mike didn't move.

Jeremy saluted, then got in the car and drove away.

"Jaguar XJS coupe, 1992," Mike said. "Only three silver cars that year. You never said your family was rich."

"He is," Tom said. "I'm not. Is it safe to go in?"

Mike mugged exasperation. "About as safe as a nuclear plant. Man, they are so fucked. Do you know how much it's worth?"

"What?"

"The car."

Tom shook his head.

"He buy you those clothes?"

Tom looked at Mike, who was suddenly thoughtful. "The haircut too."

"What a fucking weirdo," Mike said.

"You don't even know him."

Mike shook his head. "I know a fucking weirdo when I see one and he is a fucking weirdo."

Patricia had not thawed yet, so they stayed outside farting around. Mike couldn't leave the yard because he was grounded for two weeks. It made him edgy and hard to be with.

Mike went in to get them Pepsis. Tom waited at the picnic table. He saw the kitchen curtain move and felt uncomfortable, the way he had in the beginning when he'd first started hanging around with Mike and Patricia had thought he was a bad influence.

Mike came back and handed him a can. Mike popped his and chugged it in one gulp, then burped, loud and long.

"You could be a fucking foghorn," Tom said, trying to lighten the mood.

"You know my mom," Mike said, ignoring him. "She was real nice. But every night she put me in the tub and poured Lysol over me." Mike crushed the can on his knee. He burped again. "Want to stay for dinner?"

"Can't."

"Watch yourself," Mike said, with his usual zigzag logic.

Tom was glad when Jeremy showed up and honked. Mike watched him leave with such a solemn expression Tom almost laughed. As they drove away, Mike held up two fingers in a victory sign, then pointed them at his eyes. Tom grinned. He'd completely forgotten that, their secret language. Abort Mission, it meant. They're on to you.

"Jail by twenty," Jeremy said, looking in his rearview mirror.

"What?"

"Thug material if I ever saw it," Jeremy said.

"He's okay," Tom said.

Jeremy shook his head. "You won't trust me, but you'll trust that?"

He didn't want to make a big thing out of this. "Mike's a good guy."

Jeremy turned the radio on.

Tom insisted, "He's just had some bad breaks."

"Who hasn't?" Jeremy said.

Screw you too, he wanted to say. Jeremy left him off in front of the building. Tom didn't know what to think of either of them. Tired and disgusted, he went up to make himself dinner.

■■

Jeremy dragged him out of bed sometime after midnight, high and happy. Woozy, Tom tried to get out of his grip, but Jeremy dragged him into the kitchen.

"Coffee?" Jeremy said.

"What time is it?" Tom said. "Do you even know what time it is? I've got an eight—"

"Whine, whine, whine," Jeremy said. "Nope. Don't you dare leave this room. You've got to stay here and keep me company."

Tom put his head in his hands and yawned. God, the only thing worse than a drunk is a druggie.

"You've got to tell me what it feels like," Jeremy said.

"What?"

"You know."

Tom glared impatiently. "What? I'm not a mind reader."

Jeremy winked. "You know." He fell off his chair and started jerking around.

"Fuck," Tom said, starting to leave. "Fuck you."

Jeremy leaped up and blocked his way. "So? Tell me."

"Why don't you jump out that window, land on your head, and you can find out for yourself."

Jeremy whooped and ran around the kitchen.

"Fuck," Tom said, spooked. "Fuck, you're gone."

Jeremy hopped up on the counter. Suddenly he turned serious. "I dropped you on your head, you know."

Tom said, "I'm going back to bed."

"I was babysitting and I pushed you and you fell down the

stairs." Jeremy toppled over, landed with a thunk on the kitchen floor and didn't move.

"Jeremy?" Tom said. "Jeremy, quit screwing around."

Jeremy stayed sprawled where he was. Tom went over to him and nudged him with his foot.

"It's not funny, Jeremy."

Jeremy pretended to convulse. Tom left him there, thrashing on the kitchen floor, and went back to his room.

He was dozing when Jeremy hopped on him. "Say you forgive me?"

Tom tried to push him off, exasperated. "Oh, for—Jeremy, it wasn't your fault. I was epileptic way before you started babysitting me, for Christ's sake. Get off!"

"Really?" Jeremy said.

"Really," Tom said. "Now can I get back to sleep?"

Jeremy looked weepy. "You're a good kid, Tommy boy. You're a super kid."

"Yeah, yeah. I'm great. Now get off. Please. Pretty please."

"I'm going to watch out for you. Yes, I am."

"Jeremy, what the hell are you on?"

"I'm high on life!" Jeremy shouted.

"Life, huh?" Tom said.

"And you'd better listen to me," Jeremy said, his eyes narrowing. "You don't know what kind of freaks are out there. You know what they can do to you? Do you?" He put his hands around Tom's throat and squeezed just enough to make him lose his breath. "Are you going to listen to me?"

Tom nodded, trying to pry Jeremy's fingers off.

Jeremy let go. "Good. Good. No more tricks. No more

lying. Don't you go lying about me to your mother. You hear me?"

Tom rubbed his throat. "Yes."

"You be good." That said, Jeremy stumbled out of the room.

When he woke up, Jeremy was gone. Tom borrowed some tools from a neighbor. He talked the guy at the hardware store into giving him a cheap deadbolt. When his mom came she could damn well pound on the door to wake him up. He wasn't putting up with Jeremy a minute longer.

That night he woke when he heard a key in the door.

"Tom!" Jeremy shouted. "Tommy! Wake up! The door's locked. Tommy!"

He pounded on the door until one of the neighbors yelled down the hall that he was calling the police. The pounding stopped. Tom closed his eyes and exhaled a breath he hadn't known he was holding.

And that is that.

Paulina.

Tom stopped at the open gym doors, hesitating.

"What's the matter?" Mike said, jogging in place.

"It's her," Tom said, stepping back inside, out of Paulina's sight.

"Man," Mike said. "She is way too old for you."

"Do we have a problem, ladies?" Greigerson bellowed across the gym.

"No problem," Mike said cheerfully. "Just taking a breather."

"Drop and give me twenty-five. Maybe that'll improve your lung power."

Mike muttered, "What a fucking—"

"Do you have a problem with that, McConnell?"

Mike put his hands up. "No problem here, sir. You got a problem with that, Tom?"

"Nope."

"I could just as easily make it fifty, smart-ass."

Tom dropped and had done ten push-ups by the time Mike was ready to do one.

"Shit," Mike said, wiping the floor. "My new shorts too. Slow down, man, you're making me look bad."

"He's watching," Tom said, not looking at Mike.

"So? Let him. What can he do?"

"Mr. McConnell!" Greigerson bellowed. "I said give me twenty-five!"

Mike did army push-ups while Greigerson was watching and girl push-ups when he wasn't. Tom counted off his last five, then stood and shook his arms out.

"Wait for me," Mike said.

"And get another twenty-five?"

"Twenty-four, and five, and done!"

"You bullshitter," Tom said, laughing. "He's not going to believe that."

Mike grinned. When they started laps again, Greigerson said nothing.

"I can't believe you got away with it," Tom said.

"It's all in the mind," Mike said, tapping his temple.

"It's all in the bullshit, you mean."

"If you can talk, ladies, you're not going fast enough," Greigerson said as they ran by him.

"I bet he's got a swastika over his bed," Mike muttered.

When Tom passed the open gym doors, he could see Paulina looking at him. He almost dropped dead but managed just to stumble a bit and bump into Mike.

"What the hell?" Mike said.

"Look."

"What?"

"Wait till we go by again."

Tom slowed as they went past the doors. Paulina waved. She's looking for Jeremy, he thought. Come on. Breathe.

"Mazenkowski. Bizarre chick," Mike said.

Greigerson yelled at them to pick up the pace. A stitch was starting in Tom's side. He slipped outside, carefully closing the doors.

Paulina was smoking on the steps. He pushed his hair back, stopped, and was about to turn around and go inside when she looked up.

"Hi," she said.

He desperately needed to sit down. "Hi."

She held out her cigarette, offering him a drag. He shook his head. "We've probably got to run for another six hours. It'd kill me."

"If you were a girl," she said, "all you'd have to do is lean over and say, 'My cramps are totally bad today. I am, like, gushing.' Seriously, Greigerson can't take that shit." She laughed. "One month I had my period six times and he never even asked for a note."

Tom was shocked, horrified, and delighted. He was sitting there beside her and she was talking to him. She was close enough that he could see the delicate fuzz on her face. The sun made her hair glow like silk. She power sucked the cigarette down to its butt and flicked it onto the ground.

"Jeremy said you did some pot," Paulina said. "You know where I can get some?"

Tom blinked. "Pot?"

"Yeah. Just a baggie. I don't get paid this week. Just to unwind, you know."

"Sure," Tom said.

"Sure you got some or sure you like to unwind?"

"Both," Tom said.

"Can I take some off your hands?" She smiled at him and if he'd had any on him, all of it would have been hers.

"Sure," he said, amazed his voice wasn't cracking. "It's in my locker."

"Your locker?" she said incredulously. "Are you nuts? What, you want to get caught?"

Tom opened his mouth and nothing came out. He couldn't speak.

"You'll learn," she said, smiling again. "What's your last class?"

"Bio."

"Okay. I'll meet you on the drive."

Tom bit his lip. "What about Jeremy?"

"What about him?"

"Are you, um." He cleared his throat. "You know, seeing him?"

Her smile became forced. "With a little therapy he'll be capable of acting like a fucking human being."

Tom said quietly, "What did he do?"

She opened her mouth, then hesitated. "I'll tell you when you're older." She stood up and brushed herself off. "I'll wait for you at the bus stop. Don't forget the stuff." She pecked him on the lips. Her mouth was soft. He floated inside.

"Greigerson wants to see you," Mike said.

Tom touched his lips. "She likes me!" He whooped and spun around.

"Whacked," Mike said, and shook his head.

Things were better at Mike's house. Evan let him in even though Patricia's expression was ominous. He played Street Fighter II with Mike until dinnertime but decided not to test Patricia's patience and went home.

Paulina had met him at the bus stop. Tom couldn't remember what they'd talked about but she'd laughed at something he said. And then, after he gave her the pot, she'd kissed him again, in front of people. She'd said if he had any more, he could bring it to a party some friends of hers were throwing.

It was a great day. The sky was pale blue. He hadn't seen Jeremy for three days. Jeremy had paid the phone bill before he left. All they had to worry about now was Mastercard and Visa. And next month's rent. Still, they were better off than they had been. He'd had a good interview at Red Robin's for a prep cook. The guy there had known Angie, his old boss. They had talked about Chuckie's, about school, just chatted. He rolled his bike into the elevator. Someone must have mopped it, because the piss smell was gone.

"I'm home!" he called out.

"Tom!" his mother said, excited. "I've got a surprise for you!"

He left the bike where it was. "What?"

Aunt Faith and his mother were sitting together on the couch. Tom stood frozen in the entranceway.

"Thomas," Aunt Faith said. "Look how handsome you are!"

"Come kiss your aunt," his mother said.

"Aunt Faith," Tom said.

She held her arms out and he went to hug her. She was thinner than he remembered. Her hair was gray and her face had deep lines he hadn't seen before. Her head shook slightly, wobbled on her neck like it was loose.

"You look like your grandfather," Aunt Faith said.

"Jeremy flew her in," his mother said. "We're going out for dinner. All of us."

The look she gave him was hopeful.

"I've got homework," he said faintly.

"Oh, pooh," his mother said, waving her hand. "This is family!"

"You work too hard," Aunt Faith said.

Jeremy wasn't at the restaurant when they got there. Aunt Faith and his mom walked in, arms linked. Jeremy wasn't mentioned. Tom knew it was just a matter of time.

Before dessert arrived Aunt Faith went to the bathroom. His mom held his hand and said, "Faith says it really was an inheritance."

Tom stared at their hands. "Is he moving back?"

"No," she said. "No, Tommy. Faith says he's just with a bad crowd right now. I saw him today. He said he was sorry. That's a good sign, don't you think?"

He couldn't meet her eyes. She let go of his hand. "Faith says Jeremy hasn't spoken to his father in two years. They used to be so close. Your cousin's just lost and hurt right now."

"So why doesn't he call him up or something?"

"Tommy—"

"No, no, I'm serious. Why does he have to hang around here?"

His mother looked hurt. "He's *family*."

"He's got *four* brothers! Why can't he stay with one of them?"

"They were always very competitive. If you had a brother you'd know what it's like."

"What's to know? It's not like he just forgot to send you a birthday card. He's a drug dealer, Mom."

From her disappointed expression, he knew he'd pushed it too far. She was probably still thinking about a happy Hallmark Christmas back east. And now she was the heroine who'd brought Jeremy into the fold again. "I don't think he's a bad person," Tom said. I think he's a fucking lunatic, he thought.

She smiled a lopsided smile. "He is a bit of a handful, isn't he?"

"Is Aunt Faith staying with us?" Tom said.

His mother hesitated. "Yes."

"That's great." Jeremy wouldn't do anything with his own

mother in their apartment. "She can have my room. I'll take the couch. How long is she staying?"

"A week," his mother said happily.

"Tell her to stay as long as she wants."

His mom looked surprised. "Things are turning our way," she said. It was more like a question.

"Yes," Tom assured her. "They are."

When he came back from school the next day the entertainment center was once again set up in the living room.

Tom couldn't sleep that night and he couldn't concentrate enough to do homework. He couldn't stay in the apartment either. He considered taking his bike but thought that it might make too much noise and wake Aunt Faith.

He slipped out the front door and took the stairs. The halls had been repainted the halls and for a few days they'd be clean. Then Wayne or Willy would start again.

The clouds hung low. The weatherman had been promising rain for the last week but there had been only drizzle. When he was near the park, a woman yelled, "Hey, Tom!"

He didn't recognize her at first because she was blond now and wearing a tight black micro mini and a bikini top instead of her usual schoolgirl-gone-bad outfit. She waved him over to her corner. He crossed the street to say hi, happy to see her. She peeked behind him.

"Did you know you're being followed?" she said.

He whirled around. Jeremy's car was at the curb. Jeremy honked.

"Goddamn it," Tom said. He marched up to Jeremy's car

and hit the hood. Jeremy backed up. Tom stooped for a rock and threw it at the windshield. "Fuck off! Just fuck off!"

Jeremy braked, thrust his door open, and leaped out. Carefully he examined the windshield, then eyed Tom. "You don't touch my car."

"Get out of my life!"

"*Meep*-badda-*meep-meep*," Jeremy said, infuriatingly smug. "Make me."

"You seriously need help, you wacko."

"Come on, get in. It's too late for you to be wandering around by yourself. I'll give you a ride home."

"Piss on you."

"Tough guy, huh? Come on, Tommy-me-lad, let's go a few rounds. Put up your dukes!"

Tom clenched his fists, turned, and started to walk away. Jeremy revved the engine. Tom heard the car coming up behind him but he thought Jeremy would stop. Instead the car bumped him hard and he fell.

"Go home!" Jeremy yelled.

When Tom tried to stand up, his ankle gave out. He heard the door open. Jeremy stood over him.

"This kind of thing wouldn't happen if you didn't piss me off," Jeremy said, putting his arm under Tom and helping him up.

Jeremy drove him home. Tom couldn't speak. He was so furious he was shaking.

"Your mom invited me to dinner on Thursday," Jeremy said, as if everything was all right, as if he hadn't tried to run him over. "See you then!"

Tom watched Jeremy drive off. Not if I can help it.

■■

His ankle was strained and ached for the next three days. On Thursday night Tom waited outside the apartment. Jeremy buzzed up and disappeared inside. Tom climbed the stairs cautiously. He stopped in front of their door and listened. The voices were faint. They came from the kitchen.

He opened the door slowly and poked his head in. The hallway was clear and Jeremy's jacket hung neatly by the door. Soundlessly Tom pulled out the car keys.

His heart was hammering hard. He felt like he was breathing through a tube. Hard to catch his breath as he slipped back out the door and made his way downstairs.

Tom stopped at apartment 206 and knocked. Thrasher music was coming from inside. The door opened. A bald guy with a dragon tattoo on his neck scowled at him.

"Is it safe to talk?" Tom said.

"I'm not selling till I'm off parole."

Maybe this wasn't going to work. Tom swallowed. There was no going back now. He took the car keys out of his pocket. "There's a 1992 Jaguar XJS in parking space 16. Can you take care of it?"

Wayne or Willy yanked him inside and closed the door. "You the owner?"

Tom shook his head.

"You live upstairs?"

Tom nodded.

"What kind of cut you want?"

Tom said, "How much is fair?"

"Seventy-five me, twenty-five you."

Tom pretended to think about it. He was just about to agree when Wayne or Willy said, "Listen, man, I'm taking all the fucking risks here."

"It's my cousin's car. He's upstairs. The security code for the car is 1017. He'll be there for another hour or two."

Wayne or Willy chuckled. "Your cousin, hey? Fuck, you're cold, man."

Tom smiled grimly. "We all have bills to pay."

Tom opened the apartment door just as Jeremy was coming down the hallway. Shit, Tom thought, fingering the fake set of keys Wayne or Willy had given him.

Appearances, Wayne or Willy had said. You got to play the game smart.

"Hiya, kid," Jeremy said.

"Tom?" his mother said, following behind his cousin.

"Hi," Tom said, trying not to look suspicious.

"We're just about to have dinner," his mom said. "Come set the table. Jeremy, could you run down to the store and pick up some creamed corn?"

"Sure, Aunt Chrissy."

"I'll get it," Tom said quickly.

"Oh, you dawdle too much," she said.

"It's no problem," Jeremy said.

"No," Tom said. "I could use a walk."

"I don't want you to disappear," his mom said. "You're staying right here. I swear, you're a regular traveling sam these days. I never see you home anymore."

"He probably has a girlfriend," Jeremy said.

Tom's face flushed bright red and they started laughing.

"Oh-ho!" his mother said. Then she got her misty look. "My baby's growing up."

God, Tom thought, as she hugged him. Jeremy rocked on his feet, making faces at him while his mom wasn't looking.

"I've got to meet her," she said.

"She's not really a girlfriend," Tom said. "We're just friends."

"That's not what I hear," Jeremy said, smiling broadly.

"Oh?" his mom said, poking Tom in the chest. "You told *him* but you didn't tell your own mother?"

"Why don't you invite her to dinner?" Jeremy said. "We've got lots of food."

Tom shook his head, "No."

"He's ashamed of us," Jeremy said.

His mother's smile faded.

"No!" Tom said. "She really is just a friend. She's, um, at cheerleading practice."

Jeremy smirked.

His mother let go of him. "Dinner's going to get cold." She poked him again. "Take a shower first. You stink." She walked into the kitchen.

Tom stayed in the hallway with Jeremy. His cousin looked down at him benignly. "Kid, you are the worst liar on the face of the earth."

Tom wanted to ask him if he was going to take his car but didn't dare. "You think I can't take care of myself but I can."

"I think you're a smart kid who acts really stupid," Jeremy said. He reached into his jacket. He looked around. He walked back into the kitchen.

Tom took the keys out and rubbed them against his shirt

to get rid of his fingerprints. He dropped the keys on the floor under Jeremy's jacket. Then he headed straight for the bathroom and locked the door. He started up the shower, stripped, and stepped in. The hot water seared his skin. He scrubbed hard.

So Jeremy lost his car. Boo-hoo. He had money. He could buy another one.

Tom had expected to feel triumphant or at least good. He had planned to be there when Jeremy came back, frantic and mad, so that he could see his cousin's expression and savor it. Instead, he stayed in the shower long after he heard Jeremy shouting. His cousin was right. He was lousy at this kind of thing.

Two policemen came an hour later and were unsympathetic. One was short and stocky and asked all the questions. He didn't like Jeremy on sight. The feeling, Tom could see, was mutual.

"You brought a car like that into this neighborhood?" the policeman asked.

"I was visiting family," Jeremy said through clenched teeth.

Tom watched, expecting him to explode again. He'd been raging around the apartment on and off since he called the police. Aunt Faith looked blankly at the floor. His mother cried. Tom stayed in his chair and tried to be invisible.

The police left a half hour later.

"I bet you anything you'll never see that car again," the stocky policeman said. "Good thing you have insurance."

"These guys are professionals," the other one put in. It was the first thing he'd said all evening. "You're the fourth stolen vehicle we've had this week."

"Great," Jeremy said.

Aunt Faith reheated the dinner none of them had touched. They ate the meal in a silence no one tried to break.

Two days later Tom went to check the mail. One of the letters was a fat manila envelope with TOM printed on it.

When he opened it, there were seventy one-hundred-dollar bills inside. He came out of his daze sitting on the ground. Seven thousand dollars. God. He hadn't expected Wayne or Willy to come through.

He looked around to see if anyone was watching, then he quickly tucked the envelope inside his jacket.

When he got upstairs and opened the rest of the mail, he found the set of fake keys he'd left for Jeremy.

"It's not a good idea," he said.

"Oh, come on," Paulina said. "Don't tell me you're chickening out."

The house was dark in front, but the driveway was jammed with cars and empty beer cases. They went into the yard. The backdoor swung open. A woman, laughing, stumbled out and fell in a mud puddle. She laughed harder. Her friend tried to pick her up and slipped. They both sat in the mud, pointing at themselves and clutching their sides. They crawled toward each other and kissed.

"Gross," Paulina said. "Come on, come on, let's get inside before we die of pneumonia."

The heavy throb of reggae pulsed through the open door. Just as they reached it, it slammed shut. A single light bulb above the doorway lit the backyard. Paulina pounded on the door.

"Ben! Ben! Open the door!"

"Well," Tom said. "Too bad. Maybe we can come back later."

"Oh, don't party poop. He just can't hear us. Help me."

Tom knocked halfheartedly. Even though the rain was soaking his collar and dripping down his shirt, he started to smile.

"Shit," Paulina said. "Come on, open up!"

Her carefully curled hair was going flat and her eyeliner was leaking down her face in aqua streams. Her dress was becoming transparent and her nipples were hard points. Tom looked away.

The door opened and they came up against a thick wall of bodies.

"It's about fucking time," Paulina snapped, shaking her head and spraying drops of water.

Everywhere people were dancing, now to the insistent beat of a heavy metal bass. A man screamed, and the whole room started screaming. Paulina wrapped her arm around his shoulders and screamed. Tom opened his mouth but felt silly so he did nothing. Paulina kissed him, her hand cool on his neck. He put a hand on her waist and kissed her back. They were shoved together by the crowd. Paulina pushed him away.

"Kitchen," she mouthed, over the noise and music.

He followed her through the living room to the kitchen. At the stove a girl with no teeth was heating butter knives on the burners. She placed a little black-brown ball of hash at the end of each knife and handed them to people who paid her. A bald man put a hashish ball between two heated butter knives, then put the knives under his nose and inhaled deeply. Tom was watching him so intently he didn't notice a smear of chip dip on the floor and slipped. He landed against a woman with a snake wound around her neck. She licked his forehead before he could jerk away from her. A man sitting inside a freezer chest was selling booze. Paulina took a soggy fifty-dollar bill from her purse and waved it at him. She cupped her hands and made as if to swallow something. He pulled a small plastic bag from his leather vest and showed it to her. Paulina nodded and gave him the fifty.

"Can we leave now?" Tom shouted.

She shook her head and plunged into the crowd of partyers blocking the doorway. Tom went after her. The snake lady pinched him hard as he went by. Tom jumped, slapping her hand away. She stuck her tongue out and wiggled it. Paulina called him from the other side of the living room, near a set of stairs. He looked back once to see the snake lady smiling at him. The snake slithered off her shoulders then and the snake lady had to duck down and grope around the floor for it.

"Take this," Paulina said as he sat beside her on the steps. She caught his hand and put shriveled bits of black leather in it.

"This?"

"Shrooms with a kick," she said, opening her own palm

to show him that she had the same thing. She popped them in her mouth and started to chew. Tom made a face. Paulina swallowed.

"They'll totally relax you. Come on. You want to have fun, right?"

He nodded.

"These're just relaxers. You don't want them, don't take them," she said, shrugging. Her face was hard. She watched him, disapproving. He cleared his throat and popped the mushrooms in his mouth the way he'd seen her do it. They had the texture of stale beef jerky.

"Good, Tommy," she said, kissing his nose. "Tell me when you feel it working."

When she wasn't looking he spat most of it on the floor.

"Anything yet?" she said, kissing his chin.

He shook his head. He felt bad, but he didn't want to spasm all over the floor in front of her if it reacted with his medication, and he didn't want to explain it either.

"Wait a few minutes."

Paulina led him back into the center of the living room. The music changed again, to techno, something with whales in the background. He thought they might be humpbacks.

Paulina smiled at him and his heart almost stopped. She pulled him close and nibbled his earlobe, her teeth pulling on it lightly. Her tongue was warm and slippery. Then it wasn't her tongue but a slug trying to crawl into his ear, and he yanked away.

"What's wro-wrong-ong?" Paulina said.

The floor was suddenly miles away. "I think iz working." He was glad he hadn't swallowed the whole handful.

"Come on-on-on-on. Thiz away-ay."

Paulina's hair writhed. Tom touched it and she grabbed his hand and towed him up some stairs, to a room at the end of the hall.

"Leeeeave the light offff," she said, undulating.

Tom nodded, hitting his head against a wall that bent down and curved over him like a rainbow.

Paulina pulled out a bronze key and unlocked the door. She let him go in first. He drifted by her, carried on a breeze. The room was completely black, but when Tom looked up he saw a red eye watching him from a corner.

Paulina staggered in and shut the door. He heard her swearing. He squinted hard. The red eye in the corner was unblinking. Stars popped into existence on the ceiling. The moon appeared briefly, then disappeared behind the curtains.

"It's lock-ock-ocked," Paulina said loudly.

Lights flared to life. Tom couldn't stop staring at the bulb as it swayed back and forth.

"Surprise!" Jeremy was standing under the light. He pulled a string and the light went off and on like a strobe. He had his other hand on a video camera. "Bet I'm the last person you expected to see-pected-to-see-to-see."

Tom ran for the door but the floor was mud sucking at his feet. Jeremy didn't stop him. When Tom reached the door, the doorknob melted. He tried to turn it but it stretched like taffy.

"Paulina!" he shouted.

She was standing by the video camera.

"Open-pen it," Tom said.

Jeremy came up behind him and wrapped his arms around

Tom's chest. "Jesus Christ," Jeremy said. "What's the-mat-the-mat-the-matter with him?"

"Gave him gave a little something."

"You stupid bitch, stupid bitch, you know I wanted him sober." Jeremy's voice was loud and ringing, right beside his ear, a bell. "I think you'd better leave, Paulina-na-na."

She shook her head. The video camera tilted. "I want stuff, my stuff, you know, stuff. Watch the birdie, kid, the birdie."

His jacket peeled away like dead skin. Jeremy threw it and it landed on the bed behind him. Hands from nowhere reached for his shirt and Tom hit them away. The floor grabbed his shirt collar and yanked him down. Jeremy left him there, on the floor, and moved in ever so slow-mo to Paulina, who looked at him blankly, even when he smacked her against the wall and she slithered down and he kicked her head, kicked her head, and kicked her head.

"Stop!" Tom shouted, sitting up.

Jeremy picked up a pair of handcuffs and turned to Tom.

"What-at-at do-ing?" Tom said, pushing himself onto his knees.

Jeremy shoved him and the room tilted and bobbed. Tom wondered how Jeremy was standing on the wall. Jeremy put one foot against Tom's neck. "Did you-you-did-think-you-think-you could get away with it?" Jeremy lifted his foot and Tom rolled away, but when he stopped his wrists were stuck behind his back. Jeremy lit a cigarette. "Any requests, last requests?"

"Stop it!" Tom shouted.

Jeremy took a deep drag and blew the smoke in Tom's face.

Tom tried to keep in the present, tried to keep his head

from following the lights and the sounds. He knew he was in deep, too deep too far. Jeremy smoked his cigarette until it was almost gone and then he stubbed it out on Tom's shoulder.

The room went golden, went flat as a sunlit wheat field.

Tom screamed for help as Jeremy lit another cigarette and smoked it, watching him, not smiling but not looking sorry. The burn hurt. The room—he saw things on the walls, saw things on the ceiling, and heard himself screaming, "The ceiling." Jeremy butted the cigarette out on his other shoulder. It felt like someone had stretched his skin between hot knives. Jeremy started a third cigarette, which he slowly inserted up Tom's nostril.

The pain let him focus hard for a moment. He stopped screaming. He found a memory and clung to it, said, "Super. Cali. Fragi. Listic—" He panicked because it was sliding away again. He couldn't hold it. He tried again, he struggled to remember, but he kept forgetting the whole word, the word, the whole word. Jeremy was staring at Tom, at Tom who was sliding toward the ceiling until Jeremy raised his fist and brought it down like judgment.

Fourth Contact

"I'd drive you home," Jeremy said, "but I don't have a car."

Tom stayed completely still, curled up on his side on the bed.

"I know you're awake," his cousin said.

The party downstairs was slowing down. The music was still pounding through the floor but the voices had stopped. He'd come to slowly. He could remember most of what happened.

"Paulina's pissed at us," Jeremy said. "I had to give her major stuff to keep her mouth shut."

Tom's hands were still cuffed behind his back. When he was waking up he thought they were frozen together, but then, as he became more alert, he felt the metal biting into his skin.

Jeremy sighed. Tom guessed that if he wanted to he could scream loud enough to attract attention. The muted sounds of people leaving echoed through the house.

The bed shifted as Jeremy stood up. Tom tensed. Jeremy's steps went around the bed. He stopped in front of Tom.

"Open your eyes, Tommy-boy." Jeremy hit the bed near Tom's face. "Now."

Tom sprang up and rammed into Jeremy. They both fell, Jeremy grunting as they hit the floor. Then he grabbed Tom by the shoulders and rolled and it was over. Jeremy whooped, dragged him up, and shoved him down on the bed. "That's more like it!"

Tom kicked out. Jeremy danced back, delighted. "Come on, Tommy! Give it the old college try!"

Tom felt himself going under, felt the energy leaving him like a retreating tide. He pushed himself as far from Jeremy as he could and stopped, panting.

Jeremy stood watching him, hands on his hips. He frowned. "Still not talking to me?"

Tom's right eye was closed and wouldn't open. It hurt a

lot. Breathing hurt. Moving hurt. If he opened his mouth he was going to start crying, and he didn't want to give Jeremy the satisfaction.

"I've got an idea," Jeremy said. "I'm going to leave the room for a minute. Stay right where you are." He stopped. "I bet you won't. Promise me . . . no, forget it. I've got a better idea."

Jeremy reached under the bed and came back up with a long coil of rope. "We brought this too," he explained. "We were planning all sorts of things for you, Tommy-boy."

Tom, suddenly energized, tried to get off the bed again, but Jeremy caught him and tied his feet together, then tethered him to the headboard.

"Back before you know it," Jeremy said, unlocking the door, then locking it behind him.

"Fire!" Tom shouted. "Fire! Goddamn it! Fire! Help!"

He twisted his hands, remembering movies where if you just moved your hands in the right way you could get free. He wasn't getting anywhere. He wanted to go back to sleep. He wanted to have never met Jeremy, who opened the door, peeked inside, and waved a pen.

Tom scrambled as far back as the rope would let him.

"Easy," Jeremy said. "Easy. Watch. Watch me. Look." He drew something on his finger and held it up. "Hi, Tom," he said. He drew another finger puppet on his other hand and said in the high, squeaky voice, " 'Hi, Jeremy!' "

Something in him broke and he started blubbering. He wanted not to be doing it, not to be breaking, not to be amusing Jeremy, but he was doing it, and not being able to stop made him cry harder.

Jeremy sat on the edge of the bed and patted his arm. It was full-fledged bawling now. It hurt his eyes. It hurt his nose where Jeremy had burned him. He could feel the rawness. Jeremy said nothing, reached down, and lit a cigarette.

Tom froze.

After a few moments Jeremy turned to him. His expression became puzzled as he opened his mouth, then looked at his cigarette. "Jeez!" he said. He lifted his shoe, stubbing the cigarette out on his sole. "It's out! See? It's out."

The relief was so strong, Tom went under, slid from the room, out of his body, gone.

Jeremy took him to Burger King for breakfast. Jeremy ordered hash browns, a large coffee, and an apple pie. Tom had an orange juice. He felt too shaky to handle anything solid. They sat upstairs at a table by the window. Tom watched the people go by. Rush hour was starting. Jeremy reached for his pocket, saw Tom watching him, and stopped.

"I'm going to have a nic-fit soon," Jeremy said.

Tom shrugged.

Jeremy ate his hash browns instead. Tom was relieved but didn't want to show it.

He'd come awake suddenly. Jeremy had freed him while he was passed out. He'd moved them to somewhere else in the house. Jeremy had said, "You want something to eat?"

They'd taken a taxi downtown. The driver had looked at Tom, looked at Jeremy, then back at Tom again, and had said nothing for the whole trip.

Paulina had watched them leave the house. Jeremy had handed her something. The side of her head was matted with blood, but she didn't seem to care. She didn't even look at him, and after that first glance, he didn't look at her.

Tom's wrists hurt where the cuffs had scraped his skin raw. They were bruised and purple. They were sticking to his shirt. He had no idea what he was going to tell his mom.

"Guess we're even now," Jeremy said.

"Even," Tom said.

"You can help me pick out a new car tomorrow. What do you say to that? I think I'll try a Mustang this time."

"You're going to blow the rest of your money on a car?"

"You think I'd keep my money in a dinky two percent savings account? That was just the tip of the iceberg. But you'll chip in $7,000, won't you?" Jeremy pointed his stir stick at Tom. "Some advice, kid. When you pick a partner in crime, pick one who can keep his mouth shut."

"It wasn't really planned." Tom sipped at the orange juice. It stung his lip.

"There was your first mistake," Jeremy said. "Now William, Willy-boy, he had a big mouth." Jeremy grinned. "And now he has a bigger mouth. Don't worry about him. I let Paulina play with him for a while. She gave him something that made him try flying." Jeremy leaned forward, suddenly serious, and said in a hushed voice, "Between you and me, I think that girl has a few problems. You might want to ask someone else to the prom."

Tom burst out laughing. He almost lost it again, couldn't stop laughing, was so close to crying Jeremy handed him a napkin, which made him laugh harder.

People were looking at them. Tom brought himself under control. He sat back in his chair. Jeremy insisted on going downstairs and getting him a pancake. Tom waited until Jeremy was out of sight before he followed him downstairs, then ran out the door. He meant to run down Granville Street, but he had to stop and lean against a wall. He felt muddled, couldn't pull himself together enough to move.

"You just don't learn, do you?" Jeremy said.

"Getting some air," Tom said.

"Feel free, go ahead," Jeremy said, not fooled. He stood back. "Look at you. You can't even walk."

"Go fuck yourself, you hear me? Find someone else to play your fucking games, you psycho." Tom had to use the wall to keep walking straight. His vision was doubling and he knew he was going to throw up, but it didn't matter. He would get away. Jeremy couldn't watch him twenty-four hours a day.

"You can leave," Jeremy said. "But your mom's not going anywhere."

Slowly Tom turned around. The sun crawled up the sky. Traffic at the intersections snarled, cars honking. He slid down the wall and slumped on the pavement.

"We can talk about this after you've had some sleep," Jeremy said.

A taxi came up the street. Jeremy put his fingers in his mouth and let out a screeching whistle. The taxi stopped. Jeremy helped him up, put him in the backseat, then slammed the door and got in next to the driver. They were going home. Tom leaned forward, put his head in his hands, and rested.

Queen of the North

Frog Song

Whenever I see abandoned buildings, I think of our old house in the village, a rickety shack by the swamp where the frogs used to live. It's gone now. The council covered the whole area with rocks and gravel.

In my memory, the sun is setting and the frogs begin to sing. As the light shifts from yellow to orange to red, I walk down the path to the beach. The wind blows in from the channel, making the grass hiss and shiver around my legs. The tide is low and there's a strong rotting smell from the beach. Tree stumps that have been washed down the channel from the logged areas loom ahead—black, twisted silhouettes against the darkening sky.

The seiner coming down the channel is the *Queen of the North*, pale yellow with blue trim, Uncle Josh's boat. I wait on the beach. The water laps my ankles. The sound of the old diesel engine grows louder as the boat gets closer.

Usually I can will myself to move, but sometimes I'm frozen where I stand, waiting for the crew to come ashore.

The only thing my cousin Ronny didn't own was a Barbie Doll speedboat. She had the swimming pool, she had the Barbie-Goes-to-Paris carrying case, but she didn't have the boat. There was one left in Northern Drugs, nestling between the puzzles and the stuffed Garfields, but it cost sixty bucks and we were broke. I knew Ronny was going to get it. She'd already saved twenty bucks out of her allowance. Anyway, she always got everything she wanted because she was an only child and both her parents worked at the aluminum smelter. Mom knew how much I wanted it, but she said it was a toss-up between school supplies and paying bills, or wasting our money on something I'd get sick of in a few weeks.

We had a small Christmas tree. I got socks and underwear and forced a cry of surprise when I opened the package. Uncle Josh came in just as Mom was carving the turkey. He pushed a big box in my direction.

"Go on," Mom said, smiling. "It's for you."

Uncle Josh looked like a young Elvis. He had the soulful brown eyes and the thick black hair. He dressed his long, thin body in clothes with expensive labels—no Sears or Kmart for him. He smiled at me with his perfect pouty lips and bleached white teeth.

"Here you go, sweetheart," Uncle Josh said.

I didn't want it. Whatever it was, I didn't want it. He put it down in front of me. Mom must have wrapped it. She was never any good at wrapping presents. You'd think with two kids and a million Christmases behind her she'd know how to wrap a present.

"Come on, open it," Mom said.

I unwrapped it slowly, my skin crawling. Yes, it was the Barbie Doll speedboat.

My mouth smiled. We all had dinner and I pulled the wishbone with my little sister, Alice. I got the bigger piece and made a wish. Uncle Josh kissed me. Alice sulked. Uncle Josh never got her anything, and later that afternoon she screamed about it. I put the boat in my closet and didn't touch it for days.

Until Ronny came over to play. She was showing off her new set of Barbie-in-the-Ice-Capades clothes. Then I pulled out the speedboat and the look on her face was almost worth it.

My sister hated me for weeks. When I was off at soccer practice, Alice took the boat and threw it in the river. To this day, Alice doesn't know how grateful I was.

There's a dream I have sometimes. Ronny comes to visit. We go down the hallway to my room. She goes in first. I point to the closet and she eagerly opens the door. She thinks I've been lying, that I don't really have a boat. She wants proof.

When she turns to me, she looks horrified, pale and shocked. I laugh, triumphant. I reach in and stop, seeing Uncle Josh's head, arms, and legs squashed inside, severed from the rest of his body. My clothes are soaked dark red with his blood.

"Well, what do you know," I say. "Wishes do come true."

■■

Me and five chug buddies are in the Tamitik arena, in the girls' locker room under the bleachers. The hockey game is in the third period and the score is tied. The yells and shouting of the fans drown out the girl's swearing. There are four of us against her. It doesn't take long before she's on the floor trying to crawl away. I want to say I'm not part of it, but that's my foot hooking her ankle and tripping her while Ronny takes her down with a blow to the temple. She grunts. Her head makes a hollow sound when it bounces off the sink. The lights make us all look green. A cheer explodes from inside the arena. Our team has scored. The girl's now curled up under the sink and I punch her and kick her and smash her face into the floor.

My cuz Ronny had great connections. She could get hold of almost any drug you wanted. This was during her biker chick phase, when she wore tight leather skirts, teeny weeny tops, and many silver bracelets, rings, and studs. Her parents started coming down really hard on her then. I went over to her house to get high. It was okay to do it there, as long as we sprayed the living room with Lysol and opened the windows before her parents came home.

We toked up and decided to go back to my house to get some munchies. Ronny tagged along when I went up to my bedroom to get the bottle of Visine. There was an envelope on my dresser. Even before I opened it I knew it would be money. I knew who it was from.

I pulled the bills out. Ronny squealed.

"Holy sheep shit, how much is there?"

I spread the fifties out on the dresser. Two hundred and fifty dollars. I could get some flashy clothes or nice earrings with that money, if I could bring myself to touch it. Anything I bought would remind me of him.

"You want to have a party?" I said to Ronny.

"Are you serious?" she said, going bug-eyed.

I gave her the money and said make it happen. She asked who it came from, but she didn't really care. She was already making phone calls.

That weekend we had a house party in town. The house belonged to one of Ronny's biker buddies and was filled with people I knew by sight from school. As the night wore on, they came up and told me what a generous person I was. Yeah, that's me, I thought, Saint Karaoke of Good Times.

I took Ronny aside when she was drunk enough. "Ronny, I got to tell you something."

"What?" she said, blinking too fast, like she had something in her eye.

"You know where I got the money?"

She shook her head, lost her balance, blearily put her hand on my shoulder, and barfed out the window.

As I listened to her heave out her guts, I decided I didn't want to tell her after all. What was the point? She had a big mouth, and anything I told her I might as well stand on a street corner and shout to the world. What I really wanted was to have a good time and forget about the money, and after beating everyone hands down at tequila shots that's exactly what I did.

"Moooo." I copy the two aliens on *Sesame Street* mooing to a telephone. Me and Uncle Josh are watching television together. He smells faintly of the halibut he cooked for dinner. Uncle Josh undoes his pants. "Moo." I keep my eyes on the TV and say nothing as he moves toward me. I'm not a baby like Alice, who runs to Mommy about everything. When it's over he'll have treats for me. It's like when the dentist gives me extra suckers for not crying, not even when it really hurts.

I could have got my scorpion tattoo at The Body Hole, where my friends went. A perfectly groomed beautician would sit me in a black-leather dentist's chair and the tattoo artist would show me the tiny diagram on tracing paper. We'd choose the exact spot on my neck where the scorpion would go, just below the hairline where the my hair comes to a point. Techno, maybe some funky remix of Abba, would blare through the speakers as he whirred the tattoo needle's motor.

But Ronny had done her own tattoo, casually standing in front of the bathroom mirror with a short needle and permanent blue ink from a pen. She simply poked the needle in and out, added the ink, and that was that. No fuss, no muss.

So I asked her to do it for me. After all, I thought, if she could brand six marks of Satan on her own breast, she could certainly do my scorpion.

Ronny led me into the kitchen and cleared off a chair. I

twisted my hair up into a bun and held it in place. She showed me the needle, then dropped it into a pot of boiling water. She was wearing a crop top and I could see her navel ring, glowing bright gold in the slanting light of the setting sun. She was prone to lifting her shirt in front of complete strangers and telling them she'd pierced herself.

Ronny emptied the water into the sink and lifted the needle in gloved hands. I bent my head and looked down at the floor as she traced the drawing on my skin.

The needle was hot. It hurt more than I expected, a deep ache, a throbbing. I breathed through my mouth. I fought not to cry. I concentrated fiercely on not crying in front of her, and when she finished I lay very still.

"See?" Ronny said. "Nothing to it, you big baby."

When I opened my eyes and raised my head, she held one small mirror to my face and another behind me so I could see her work. I frowned at my reflection. The scorpion looked like a smear.

"It'll look better when the swelling goes down," she said, handing me the two mirrors.

As Ronny went to start the kettle for tea, she looked out the window over the sink. "Star light, star bright, first star—"

I glanced out the window. "That's Venus."

"Like you'd know the difference."

I didn't want to argue. The skin on the back of my neck ached like it was sunburned.

I am singing Janis Joplin songs, my arms wrapped around the karaoke machine. I fend people off with a stolen switchblade.

No one can get near until some kid from school has the bright idea of giving me drinks until I pass out.

Someone else videotapes me so my one night as a rock star is recorded forever. She tries to send it to *America's Funniest Home Videos*, but they reject it as unsuitable for family viewing. I remember nothing else about that night after I got my first hit of acid. My real name is Adelaine, but the next day a girl from school sees me coming and yells, "Hey, look, it's Karaoke!"

The morning after my sixteenth birthday I woke up looking down into Jimmy Hill's face. We were squashed together in the backseat of a car and I thought, God, I didn't.

I crawled around and found my shirt and then spent the next half hour vomiting beside the car. I vaguely remembered the night before, leaving the party with Jimmy. I remembered being afraid of bears.

Jimmy stayed passed out in the backseat, naked except for his socks. We were somewhere up in the mountains, just off a logging road. The sky was misty and gray. As I stood up and stretched, the car headlights went out.

Dead battery. That's just fucking perfect, I thought.

I checked the trunk and found an emergency kit. I got out one of those blankets that look like a large sheet of aluminum and wrapped it around myself. I searched the car until I found my jeans. I threw Jimmy's shirt over him. His jeans were hanging off the car's antenna. When I took them down, the antenna wouldn't straighten up.

I sat in the front seat. I had just slept with Jimmy Hill.

Christ, he was practically a Boy Scout. I saw his picture in the local newspaper all the time, with these medals for swimming. Other than that, I never really noticed him. We went to different parties.

About midmorning, the sun broke through the mist and streamed to the ground in fingers of light, just like in the movies when God is talking to someone. The sun hit my face and I closed my eyes.

I heard the seat shift and turned. Jimmy smiled at me and I knew why I'd slept with him. He leaned forward and we kissed. His lips were soft and the kiss was gentle. He put his hand on the back of my neck. "You're beautiful."

I thought it was just a line, the polite thing to say after a one-night stand, so I didn't answer.

"Did you get any?" Jimmy said.

"What?" I said.

"Blueberries." He grinned. "Don't you remember?"

I stared at him.

His grin faded. "Do you remember anything?"

I shrugged.

"Well. We left the party, I dunno, around two, I guess. You said you wanted blueberries. We came out here—" He cleared his throat.

"Then we fucked, passed out, and now we're stranded." I finished the sentence. The sun was getting uncomfortable. I took off the emergency blanket. I had no idea what to say next. "Battery's dead."

He swore and leaned over me to try the ignition.

I got out of his way by stepping out of the car. Hastily he

put his shirt on, not looking up at me. He had a nice chest, buff and tan. He blushed and I wondered if he had done this before.

"You cool with this?" I said.

He immediately became macho. "Yeah."

I felt really shitty then. God, I thought, he's going to be a bragger.

I went and sat on the hood. It was hot. I was thirsty and had a killer headache. Jimmy got out and sat beside me.

"You know where we are?" Jimmy said.

"Not a fucking clue."

He looked at me and we both started laughing.

"You were navigating last night," he said, nudging me.

"You always listen to pissed women?"

"Yeah," he said, looking sheepish. "Well. You hungry?"

I shook my head. "Thirsty."

Jimmy hopped off the car and came back with a warm Coke from under the driver's seat. We drank it in silence.

"You in any rush to get back?" he asked.

We started laughing again and then went hunting for blueberries. Jimmy found a patch not far from the car and we picked the bushes clean. I'd forgotten how tart wild blueberries are. They're smaller than store-bought berries, but their flavor is much more intense.

"My sister's the wilderness freak," Jimmy said. "She'd be able to get us out of this. Or at least she'd know where we are."

We were perched on a log. "You gotta promise me something."

"What?"

"If I pop off before you, you aren't going to eat me."

"What?"

"I'm serious," I said. "And I'm not eating any bugs."

"If you don't try them, you'll never know what you're missing." Jimmy looked at the road. "You want to pick a direction?'

The thought of trekking down the dusty logging road in the wrong direction held no appeal to me. I must have made a face because Jimmy said, "Me neither."

After the sun set, Jimmy made a fire in front of the car. We put the aluminum blanket under us and lay down. Jimmy pointed at the sky. "That's the Big Dipper."

"Ursa Major," I said. "Mother of all bears. There's Ursa Minor, Cassiopeia . . ." I stopped.

"I didn't know you liked astronomy."

"It's pretty nerdy."

He kissed me. "Only if you think it is." He put his arm around me and I put my head on his chest and listened to his heart. It was a nice way to fall asleep.

Jimmy shook me awake. "Car's coming." He pulled me to my feet. "It's my sister."

"Mmm." Blurrily I focused on the road. I could hear birds and, in the distance, the rumble of an engine.

"My sister could find me in hell," he said.

When they dropped me off at home, my mom went ballistic. "Where the hell were you?"

"Out." I stopped at the door. I hadn't expected her to be there when I came in.

Her chest was heaving. I thought she'd start yelling, but she said very calmly, "You've been gone for two days."

You noticed? I didn't say it. I felt ill and I didn't want a fight. "Sorry. Should've called."

I pushed past her, kicked off my shoes, and went upstairs.

Still wearing my smelly jeans and shirt I lay down on the bed. Mom followed me to my room and shook my shoulder.

"Tell me where you've been."

"At Ronny's."

"Don't lie to me. What is wrong with you?"

God. Just get lost. I wondered what she'd do if I came out and said what we both knew. Probably have a heart attack. Or call me a liar.

"You figure it out," I said. "I'm going to sleep." I expected her to give me a lecture or something, but she just left.

Sometimes, when friends were over, she'd point to Alice and say, "This is my good kid." Then she'd point to me and say, "This is my rotten kid, nothing but trouble. She steals, she lies, she sleeps around. She's just no damn good."

Alice knocked on my door later.

"Fuck off," I said.

"You've got a phone call."

"Take a message. I'm sleeping."

Alice opened the door and poked her head in. "You want me to tell Jimmy anything else?"

I scrambled down the hallway and grabbed the receiver. I took a couple of deep breaths so it wouldn't sound like I'd rushed to the phone. "Hi."

"Hi," Jimmy said. "We just replaced the battery on the car. You want to go for a ride?"

"Aren't you grounded?"

He laughed. "So?"

I thought he just wanted to get lucky again, and then I thought, What the hell, at least this time I'll remember it.

"Pick me up in five minutes."

I'm getting my ass kicked by two sisters. They're really good. They hit solidly and back off quickly. I don't even see them coming anymore. I get mad enough to kick out. By sheer luck, the kick connects. One of the sisters shrieks and goes down. She's on the ground, her leg at an odd angle. The other one loses it and swings. The bouncer steps in and the crowd around us boos.

"My cousins'll be at a biker party. You want to go?"

Jimmy looked at me like he wasn't sure if I was serious.

"I'll be good," I said, crossing my heart then holding up my fingers in a scout salute.

"What fun would that be?" he said, revving the car's engine.

I gave him directions. The car roared away from our house, skidding a bit. Jimmy didn't say anything. I found it unnerving. He looked over at me, smiled, then turned back to face the road. I was used to yappy guys, but this was nice. I leaned my head back into the seat. The leather creaked.

Ronny's newest party house didn't look too bad, which could have meant it was going to be dead in there. It's hard to get down and dirty when you're worried you'll stain the carpet. You couldn't hear anything thing until someone opened the door and the music throbbed out. They did a good job with the soundproofing. We went up the steps just as my cousin Frank came out with some bar buddies.

Jimmy stopped when he saw Frank and I guess I could see why. Frank is on the large side, six-foot-four and scarred up from his days as a hard-core Bruce Lee fan, when he felt compelled to fight Evil in street bars. He looked down at Jimmy.

"Hey, Jimbo," Frank said. "Heard you quit the swim team."

"You betcha," Jimmy said.

"Fucking right!" Frank body-slammed him. He tended to be more enthusiastic than most people could handle, but Jimmy looked okay with it. "More time to party," he said. Now they were going to gossip forever so I went inside.

The place was half-empty. I recognized some people and nodded. They nodded back. The music was too loud for conversation.

"You want a drink?" Frank yelled, touching my arm.

I jumped. He quickly took his hand back. "Where's Jimmy?"

"Ronny gave him a hoot and now he's hacking up his lungs out back." Frank took off his jacket, closed his eyes, and shuffled back and forth. All he knew was the reservation two-step and I wasn't in the mood. I moved toward the porch but Frank grabbed my hand. "You two doing the wild thing?"

"He's all yours," I said.

"Fuck you," Frank called after me.

Jimmy was leaning against the railing, his back toward me, his hands jammed into his pockets. I watched him. His hair was dark and shiny, brushing his shoulders. I liked the way he moved, easily, like he was in no hurry to get anywhere. His eyes were light brown with gold flecks. I knew that in a moment he would turn and smile at me and it would be like stepping into sunlight.

In my dream Jimmy's casting a fishing rod. I'm afraid of getting hooked, so I sit at the bow of the skiff. The ocean is mildly choppy, the sky is hard blue, the air is cool. Jimmy reaches over to kiss me, but now he is soaking wet. His hands and lips are cold, his eyes are sunken and dull. Something moves in his mouth. It isn't his tongue. When I pull away, a crab drops from his lips and Jimmy laughs. "Miss me?"

I feel a scream in my throat but nothing comes out.

"What's the matter?" Jimmy tilts his head. Water runs off his hair and drips into the boat. "Crab got your tongue?"

This one's outside Hanky Panky's. The woman is so totally bigger than me it isn't funny. Still, she doesn't like getting hurt. She's afraid of the pain but can't back down because she started it. She's grabbing my hair, yanking it hard. I pull hers. We get stuck there, bent over, trying to kick each other, neither one of us willing to let go. My friends are laughing their heads off. I'm pissed at that but I'm too sloshed to let go. In the morning my scalp will throb and be so tender I won't be able to comb my hair. At that moment, a bouncer comes over and splits us apart. The woman tries to kick me but kicks him instead and he knocks her down. My friends grab my arm and steer me to the bus stop.

Jimmy and I lay down together on a sleeping bag in a field of fireweed. The forest fire the year before had razed the place and the weeds had only sprouted back up about a month earlier. With the spring sun and just the right sprinkling of rain, they were as tall as sunflowers, as dark pink as prize roses, swaying around us in the night breeze.

Jimmy popped open a bottle of Baby Duck. "May I?" he said, reaching down to untie my sneaker.

"You may," I said.

He carefully lifted the sneaker and poured in some Baby Duck. Then he raised it to my lips and I drank. We lay down, flattening fireweed and knocking over the bottle. Jimmy nibbled my ear. I drew circles in the bend of his arm. Headlights came up fast, then disappeared down the highway. We watched the fireweed shimmer and wave in the wind.

"You're quiet tonight," Jimmy said. "What're you thinking?"

I almost told him then. I wanted to tell him. I wanted someone else to know and not have it locked inside me. I kept starting and then chickening out. What was the point? He'd probably pull away from me in horror, disgusted, revolted.

"I want to ask you something," Jimmy whispered. I closed my eyes, feeling my chest tighten. "You hungry? I've got a monster craving for chicken wings."

Bloody Vancouver

When I got to Aunt Erma's the light in the hallway was going spastic, flickering like a strobe, little bright flashes then darkness so deep I had to feel my way along the wall. I stopped in front of the door, sweating, smelling myself through the thick layer of deodorant. I felt my stomach go queasy and wondered if I was going to throw up after all. I hadn't eaten and was still bleeding heavily.

Aunt Erma lived in east Van in a low-income government housing unit. Light showed under the door. I knocked. I could hear the familiar opening of *Star Trek*, the old version, with the trumpets blaring. I knocked again.

The door swung open and a girl with a purple mohawk and Cleopatra eyeliner thrust money at me.

"Shit," she said. She looked me up and down, pulling the money back. "Where's the pizza?"

"I'm sorry," I said. "I think I have the wrong house."

"Pizza, pizza, pizza!" teenaged voices inside screamed. Someone was banging the floor in time to the chant.

"You with Cola?" she asked me.

I shook my head. "No. I'm here to see Erma Williamson. Is she in?"

"In? I guess. Mom?" she screamed. "Mom? It's for you!"

A whoop rose up. "Erma and Marley sittin' in a tree, k-i-s-s-i-n-g. First comes lust—"

"Shut up, you social rejects!"

"—then comes humping, then comes a baby after all that bumping!"

"How many times did they boink last night!" a single voice yelled over the laughter.

"Ten!" the voices chorused enthusiastically. "Twenty! Thirty! Forty!"

"Hey! Who's buying the pizza, eh? No respect! I get no respect!"

Aunt Erma came to the door. She didn't look much different from her pictures, except she wasn't wearing her cat-eye glasses.

She stared at me, puzzled. Then she spread open her arms.

"Adelaine, baby! I wasn't expecting you! Hey, come on in and say hi to your cousins. Pepsi! Cola! Look who came by for your birthday!"

She gave me a tight bear hug and I wanted to cry.

Two girls stood at the entrance to the living room, identical right down to their lip rings. They had different colored Mohawks though—one pink, one purple.

"Erica?" I said, peering. I vaguely remembered them as having pigtails and making fun of Mr. Rogers. "Heather?"

"It's Pepsi," the purple Mohawk said. "Not, n-o-t, Erica."

"Oh," I said.

"Cola," the pink-Mohawked girl said, turning around and ignoring me to watch TV.

"What'd you bring us?" Pepsi said matter-of-factly.

"Excuse the fruit of my loins," Aunt Erma said, leading me into the living room and sitting me between two guys who were glued to the TV. "They've temporarily lost their manners. I'm putting it down to hormones and hoping the birth control pills turn them back into normal human beings."

Aunt Erma introduced me to everyone in the room, but their names went in one ear and out the other. I was so relieved just to be there and out of the clinic I couldn't concentrate on much else.

"How is he, Bones?" the guy on my right said, exactly in synch with Captain Kirk on TV. Captain Kirk was standing over McCoy and a prone security guard with large purple circles all over his face.

"He's dead, Jim," the guy on my left said.

"I wanna watch something else," Pepsi said. "This sucks."
She was booed.

"Hey, it's my birthday. I can watch what I want."

"Siddown," Cola said. "You're out-voted."

"You guys have no taste at all. This is crap. I just can't believe you guys are watching this—this cultural pabulum. I—"

A pair of panties hit her in the face. The doorbell rang and the pink-haired girl held the pizza boxes over her head and yelled, "Dinner's ready!"

"Eat in the kitchen," Aunt Erma said. "All of youse. I ain't scraping your cheese out of my carpet."

Everyone left except me and Pepsi. She grabbed the remote control and flipped through a bunch of channels until we arrived at one where an announcer for the World Wrestling Federation screamed that the ref was blind.

"Now this," Pepsi said, "is entertainment."

By the time the party ended, I was snoring on the couch. Pepsi shook my shoulder. She and Cola were watching Bugs Bunny and Tweety.

"If we're bothering you," Cola said. "You can go crash in my room."

"Thanks," I said. I rolled off the couch, grabbed my backpack, and found the bathroom on the second floor. I made it just in time to throw up in the sink. The cramps didn't come back as badly as on the bus, but I took three Extra-Strength

Tylenols anyway. My pad had soaked right through and leaked all over my underwear. I put on clean clothes and crashed in one of the beds. I wanted a black hole to open up and suck me out of the universe.

When I woke, I discovered I should have put on a diaper. It looked like something had been hideously murdered on the mattress.

"God," I said just as Pepsi walked in. I snatched up the blanket and tried to cover the mess.

"Man," Pepsi said. "Who are you? Carrie?"

"Freaky," Cola said, coming in behind her. "You okay?"

I nodded. I wished I'd never been born.

Pepsi hit my hand when I touched the sheets. "You're not the only one with killer periods." She pushed me out of the bedroom. In the bathroom she started water going in the tub for me, poured some Mr. Bubble in, and left without saying anything. I stripped off my blood-soaked underwear and hid them in the bottom of the garbage. There would be no saving them. I lay back. The bubbles popped and gradually the water became cool. I was smelly and gross. I scrubbed hard but the smell wouldn't go away.

"You still alive in there?" Pepsi said, opening the door.

I jumped up and whisked the shower curtain shut.

"Jesus, don't you knock?"

"Well, excuuuse me. I brought you a bathrobe. Good thing you finally crawled out of bed. Mom told us to make you eat something before we left. We got Ichiban, Kraft, or hot dogs. You want anything else, you gotta make it yourself. What do you want?"

"Privacy."

"We got Ichiban, Kraft, or hot dogs. What do you want?"

"The noodles," I said, more to get her out than because I was hungry.

She left and I tried to lock the door. It wouldn't lock so I scrubbed myself off quickly. I stopped when I saw the bathwater. It was dark pink with blood.

I crashed on the couch and woke when I heard sirens. I hobbled to the front window in time to see an ambulance pull into the parking lot. The attendants wheeled a man bound to a stretcher across the lot. He was screaming about the eyes in the walls that were watching him, waiting for him to fall asleep so they could come peel his skin from his body.

Aunt Erma, the twins, and I drove to the powwow at the Trout Lake community center in East Vancouver. I was still bleeding a little and felt pretty lousy, but Aunt Erma was doing fundraising for the Helping Hands Society and had asked me to work her bannock booth. I wanted to help her out.

Pepsi had come along just to meet guys, dressed up in her flashiest bracelets and most conservatively ripped jeans. Aunt Erma enlisted her too, when she found out that none of her other volunteers had showed up. Pepsi was disgusted.

Cola got out of working at the booth because she was one of the jingle dancers. Aunt Erma had made her outfit, a form-fitting red dress with silver jingles that flashed and twinkled as she walked. Cola wore a bobbed wig to cover her pink mowhawk. Pepsi bugged her about it, but Cola airily waved good-bye and said, "Have fun."

I hadn't made fry bread in a long time. The first three batches were already mixed. I just added water and kneaded them into shapes roughly the size of a large doughnut, then threw them in the electric frying pan. The oil spattered and crackled and steamed because I'd turned the heat up too high. Pepsi wasn't much better. She burned her first batch and then had to leave so she could watch Cola dance.

"Be right back," she said. She gave me a thumbs-up sign and disappeared into the crowd.

The heat from the frying pan and the sun was fierce. I wished I'd thought to bring an umbrella. One of the organizers gave me her baseball cap. Someone else brought me a glass of water. I wondered how much longer Pepsi was going to be. My arms were starting to hurt.

I flattened six more pieces of bread into shape and threw them in the pan, beyond caring anymore that none of them were symmetrical. I could feel the sun sizzling my forearms, my hands, my neck, my legs. A headache throbbed at the base of my skull.

The people came in swarms, buzzing groups of tourists, conventioneers on a break, families, and assorted browsers. Six women wearing HI! MY NAME IS tags stopped and bought all the fry bread I had. Another hoard came and a line started at my end of the table.

"Last batch!" I shouted to the cashiers. They waved at me.

"What are you making?" someone asked.

I looked up. A middle-aged red-headed man in a business suit stared at me. At the beginning, when we were still feeling spunky, Pepsi and I had had fun with that question. We said, Oh, this is fish-head bread. Or fried beer foam. But bull-shitting took energy.

"Fry bread," I said. "This is my last batch."

"Is it good?"

"I don't think you'll find out," I said. "It's all gone."

The man looked at my tray. "There seems to be more than enough. Do I buy it from you?"

"No, the cashier, but you're out of luck, it's all sold." I pointed to the line of people.

"Do you do this for a living?" the man said.

"Volunteer work. Raising money for the Helping Hands," I said.

"Are you Indian then?"

A hundred stupid answers came to my head but like I said, bullshit is work. "Haisla. And you?"

He blinked. "Is that a tribe?"

"Excuse me," I said, taking the fry bread out of the pan and passing it down to the cashier.

The man slapped a twenty-dollar bill on the table. "Make another batch."

"I'm tired," I said.

He put down another twenty.

"You don't understand. I've been doing this since this morning. You could put a million bucks on the table and I wouldn't change my mind."

He put five twenty-dollar bills on the table.

It was all for the Helping Hands, I figured, and he wasn't going to budge. I emptied the flour bag into the bowl. I measured out a handful of baking powder, a few fingers of salt, a thumb of lard. Sweat dribbled over my face, down the tip of my nose, and into the mix as I kneaded the dough until it was very soft but hard to shape. For a hundred bucks I made sure the pieces of fry bread were roughly the same shape.

"You have strong hands," the man said.

"I'm selling fry bread."

"Of course."

I could feel him watching me, was suddenly aware of how far my shirt dipped and how short my cutoffs were. In the heat, they were necessary. I was sweating too much to wear anything more.

"My name is Arnold," he said.

"Pleased to meet you, Arnold," I said. "Scuse me if I don't shake hands. You with the convention?"

"No. I'm here on vacation."

He had teeth so perfect I wondered if they were dentures. No, probably caps. I bet he took exquisite care of his teeth.

We said nothing more until I'd fried the last piece of bread. I handed him the plate and bowed. I expected him to leave then, but he bowed back and said, "Thank you."

"No," I said. "Thank you. The money's going to a good cause. It'll—"

"How should I eat these?" he interrupted me.

With your mouth, asshole. "Put some syrup on them, or jam, or honey. Anything you want."

"Anything?" he said, staring deep into my eyes.

Oh, barf. "Whatever."

I wiped sweat off my forehead with the back of my hand, reached down and unplugged the frying pan. I began to clean up, knowing that he was still standing there, watching.

"What's your name?" he said.

"Suzy," I lied.

"Why're you so pale?"

I didn't answer. He blushed suddenly and cleared his throat. "Would you do me a favor?"

"Depends."

"Would you—" he blushed harder, "shake your hair out of that baseball cap?"

I shrugged, pulled the cap off, and let my hair loose. It hung limply down to my waist. My scalp felt like it was oozing enough oil to cause environmental damage.

"You should keep it down at all times," he said.

"Good-bye, Arnold," I said, picking up the money and starting toward the cashiers. He said something else but I kept on walking until I reached Pepsi.

I heard the buzz of an electric razor. Aunt Erma hated it when Pepsi shaved her head in the bedroom. She came out of her room, crossed the landing, and banged on the door. "In the bathroom!" she shouted. "You want to get hair all over the rug?"

The razor stopped. Pepsi ripped the door open and stomped down the hall. She kicked the bathroom door shut and the buzz started again.

I went into the kitchen and popped myself another Jolt. Sweat trickled down my pits, down my back, ran along my jaw and dripped off my chin.

"Karaoke?" Pepsi said. Then louder. "Hey! Are you deaf?"

"What?" I said.

"Get me my cell phone."

"Why don't you get it?"

"I'm on the can."

"So?" Personally, I hate it when you're talking on the phone with someone and then you hear the toilet flush.

Pepsi banged about in the bathroom and came out with her freshly coiffed Mohawk and her backpack slung over her shoulder. "What's up your butt?" she said.

"Do you want me to leave? Is that it?"

"Do what you want. This place is like an oven," Pepsi said. "Who can deal with this bullshit?" She slammed the front door behind her.

The apartment was quiet now, except for the chirpy weatherman on the TV promising another week of record highs. I moved out to the balcony. The headlights from the traffic cut into my eyes, bright and painful. Cola and Aunt Erma bumped around upstairs, then their bedroom doors squeaked shut and I was alone. I had a severe caffeine buzz. Shaky hands, fluttery heart, mild headache. It was still warm outside, heat rising from the concrete, stored up during the last four weeks of weather straight from hell. I could feel my eyes itching. This was the third night I was having trouble getting to sleep.

Tired and wired. I used to be able to party for days and days. You start to hallucinate badly after the fifth day without sleep. I don't know why, but I used to see leprechauns. These waist-high men would come and sit beside me, smiling with their brown wrinkled faces, brown eyes, brown teeth. When I tried to shoo them away, they'd leap straight up into the air, ten or twelve feet, their green clothes and long red hair flapping around them.

A low, gray haze hung over Vancouver, fuzzing the street

lights. Air-quality bulletins on the TV were warning the elderly and those with breathing problems to stay indoors. There were mostly semis on the roads this late. Their engines rumbled down the street, creating minor earthquakes. Pictures trembled on the wall. I took a sip of warm, flat Jolt, let it slide over my tongue, sweet and harsh. It had a metallic twang, which meant I'd drunk too much, my stomach wanted to heave.

I went back inside and started to pack.

Home Again, Home Again, Jiggity-Jig

Jimmy and I lay in the graveyard, on one of my cousin's graves. We should have been creeped out, but we were both tipsy.

"I'm never going to leave the village," Jimmy said. His voice buzzed in my ears.

"Mmm."

"Did you hear me?" Jimmy said.

"Mmm."

"Don't you care?" Jimmy said, sounding like I should.

"This is what we've got, and it's not that bad."

He closed his eyes. "No, it's not bad."

I poured myself some cereal. Mom turned the radio up. She glared at me as if it were my fault the Rice Crispies were loud. I opened my mouth and kept chewing.

The radio announcer had a thick Nisga'a accent. Most of the news was about the latest soccer tournament. I thought, that's northern native broadcasting: sports or bingo.

"Who's this?" I said to Mom. I'd been rummaging through the drawer, hunting for spare change.

"What?"

It was the first thing she'd said to me since I'd come back. I'd heard that she'd cried to practically everyone in the village, saying I'd gone to Vancouver to become a hooker.

I held up a picture of a priest with his hand on a little boy's shoulder. The boy looked happy.

"Oh, that," Mom said. "I forgot I had it. He was Uncle Josh's teacher."

I turned it over. *Dear Joshua*, it read. *How are you? I miss you terribly. Please write. Your friend in Christ, Archibald.*

"Looks like he taught him more than just prayers."

"What are you talking about? Your Uncle Josh was a bright student. They were fond of each other."

"I bet," I said, vaguely remembering that famous priest who got eleven years in jail. He'd molested twenty-three boys while they were in residential school.

Uncle Josh was home from fishing for only two more days. As he was opening my bedroom door, I said, "Father Archibald?"

He stopped. I couldn't see his face because of the way the light was shining through the door. He stayed there a long time.

"I've said my prayers," I said.

He backed away and closed the door.

In the kitchen the next morning he wouldn't look at me.

I felt light and giddy, not believing it could end so easily. Before I ate breakfast I closed my eyes and said grace out loud. I had hardly begun when I heard Uncle Josh's chair scrape the floor as he pushed it back.

I opened my eyes. Mom was staring at me. From her expression I knew that she knew. I thought she'd say something then, but we ate breakfast in silence.

"Don't forget your lunch," she said.

She handed me my lunch bag and went up to her bedroom.

I use a recent picture of Uncle Josh that I raided from Mom's album. I paste his face onto the body of Father Archibald and my face onto the boy. The montage looks real enough. Uncle Josh is smiling down at a younger version of me.

My period is vicious this month. I've got clots the size and texture of liver. I put one of them in a Ziploc bag. I put the picture and the bag in a hatbox. I tie it up with a bright red ribbon. I place it on the kitchen table and go upstairs to get a jacket. I think nothing of leaving it there because there's no one else at home. The note inside the box reads, "It was yours so I killed it."

"Yowtz!" Jimmy called out as he opened the front door. He came to my house while I was upstairs getting my jacket. He was going to surprise me and take me to the hot springs. I stopped at the top of the landing. Jimmy was sitting at the kitchen table with the present that I'd meant for Uncle Josh, looking at the note. Without seeing me, he closed the box, neatly folded the note, and walked out the door.

■■

He wouldn't take my calls. After two days, I went over to Jimmy's house, my heart hammering so hard I could feel it in my temples. Michelle answered the door.

"Karaoke!" she said, smiling. Then she frowned. "He's not here. Didn't he tell you?"

"Tell me what?"

"He got the job," Michelle said.

My relief was so strong I almost passed out. "A job."

"I know. I couldn't believe it either. It's hard to believe he's going fishing, he's so spoiled. I think he'll last a week. Thanks for putting in a good word, anyways." She kept talking, kept saying things about the boat.

My tongue stuck in my mouth. My feet felt like two slabs of stone. "So he's on *Queen of the North*?"

"Of course, silly," Michelle said. "We know you pulled strings. How else could Jimmy get on with your uncle?"

The lunchtime buzzer rings as I smash this girl's face. Her front teeth crack. She screams, holding her mouth as blood spurts from her split lips. The other two twist my arms back and hold me still while the fourth one starts smacking my face, girl hits, movie hits. I aim a kick at her crotch. The kids around us cheer enthusiastically. She rams into me and I go down as someone else boots me in the kidneys.

I hide in the bushes near the docks and wait all night. Near sunrise, the crew starts to make their way to the boat. Uncle Josh arrives first, throwing his gear onto the deck, then dragging it inside the cabin. I see Jimmy carrying two heavy bags. As he walks down the gangplank, his footsteps make hollow thumping noises that echo off the mountains. The docks creak, seagulls circle overhead in the soft morning light, and the smell of the beach at low tide is carried on the breeze that ruffles the water. When the seiner's engines start, Jimmy passes his bags to Uncle Josh, then unties the rope and casts off. Uncle Josh holds out his hand, Jimmy takes it and is pulled on board. The boat chugs out of the bay and rounds the point. I come out of the bushes and stand on the dock, watching the *Queen of the North* disappear.